Cry of the Eagle

by Billie Touchstone Signer
illustrations by Bob Bliss

BOOKS & MEDIA
BOSTON

Library of Congress Cataloging-in-Publication Data

Signer, Billie Touchstone, 1930-
    Cry of the eagle / written by Billie Touchstone Signer ;
    illustrated by Bob Bliss.
        p.   cm.
    ISBN 0-8198-1455-5 (pbk.)
    1. United States—History—Revolution, 1775-1783—Juvenile
fiction.   [1. United States—History—Revolution, 1775-1783—
Fiction.] I. Bliss, Bob, 1945-   ill. II. Title.
PZ7.S578Cr   1990
[Fic]—dc19   88-18500
                                                   CIP
                                                   AC

Printed and published in the U.S.A. by Pauline Books & Media, 50 St.
Paul's Avenue, Boston, MA 02130.

Pauline Books & Media is the publishing house of the Daughters of
St. Paul, an international congregation of women religious serving the
Church with the communications media.

2 3 4 5 6   99 98 97 96

*To John, who makes
the sun come up
in my heart...*

Contents

CHAPTER ONE

1776

Willie held the axe in mid-air over the log and listened. The Indian half of him sensed danger. Horsemen were coming into the narrow valley!

He dropped the axe and ran inside the log house where his grandfather was bent near the fireplace stirring a pot of stew.

"Riders coming. Sounds like at least three!"

The old man looked up at his tall grandson and frowned. "Get my rifle."

In one swift motion, Willie took the long gun from over the fireplace and checked it.

Satisfied that it was ready, he followed his grandfather onto the porch. The thumping in his heart reminded him of the drums in his mother's Indian village.

Pieter Krol squinted into the brightness of the snow-covered valley to recognize the riders rounding the curve in the wagon road.

The war for freedom made them ever cautious. The intruders could be Indians, a British scouting party or thieving Tories.

Suddenly, a wild turkey call rippled over the valley. A slow smile crossed Willie's face. "It's Vater and two others." He often used the Dutch word for *father.*

Pieter sighed with relief. The wild turkey call was their signal.

They walked out into the yard. Willie relaxed his grip on the rifle, then quickly sucked in his breath as the riders came into view. "Vater's hurt!"

The other two riders—young men—quickly dismounted and helped Karl from his horse.

Karl smiled at his son. "I'm all right. Just a flesh wound." He used his good arm to hug Willie's shoulder.

The boy then touched his father's arm. "Are you sure, Vater?"

"Yeah, just weary of getting scared out of my wits so much."

The group chuckled, and Karl made introductions. "Phillip Walters and his cousin, Jon Walters, meet my family. My father, the ornery old Dutchman, and my son, William, called Willie for short."

He tousled Willie's dark hair and smiled. The boy felt uncomfortable under their gaze.

Karl understood and added, "My son is half Seneca Indian; my wife, God rest her soul, was the daughter of a chief. A finer woman never lived."

Willie warmed at those words. Though he had been only twelve when a cruel fever took his mother's life, he knew that his parents had loved each other dearly.

The young men smiled and Jon said, "It's a pleasure to meet you both." Their breath came out like smoke in the cold air.

"Let's go in and warm ourselves, fellows." Karl put his arm around Willie's shoulder.

Phillip said, "We got to git along, Karl. Take care of that arm."

"I will, and thanks for seeing me home. I'll be getting on with my errand after I doctor my arm."

Jon said, "Well, don't rush too much. A couple of days can't make that much difference."

They waved good-bye as Willie handed his grandfather the rifle and headed for the stable with his father's horse.

———————

After Willie had dressed the wound and the Krols had eaten their stew, Karl propped himself up on a pillow near the fire. Just as he cleared his throat, the older man leaned forward in his rocker. "Vell, Karl, vat did you do? Try to take the British army on single-handed?"

Willie grinned. "He could have."

Grandfather looked quickly at the boy and chuckled. "You tink he can valk on vatter, you do."

The boy sat crosslegged on the rough floor. "He could if he wanted to." He looked at his father. Karl was blind in one eye from a hunting accident, but Willie still thought him handsome in a rough sort of way.

Karl pretended to be hurt. "You two knotheads want to hear my story or not?"

They gave him their full attention.

"Well, me and those two Walters fellows were sneaking around to check on a Tory outfit that's been doing a lot of mean things. We found 'em near the kill* the other side of Wilton, pow-wowing with three Mohawks." Karl sighed. "Wouldn't you know, about that time, Jon had a coughing fit. They heard and started firing like a bunch of nitwits. We took cover and returned their fire. They scampered in every direction 'cause they didn't know how many we were. Then I caught a little old ball, but it went clean through." He looked at his bandaged arm and winced.

———————

*kill—creek

Willie knew the wound was much more than Karl made out. He had helped his father to dress the ugly wound, putting bear grease and pitch on it.

Pieter fussed over his son. "You need to be in bed under the covers. Let me help you off the floor."

Karl grinned as he accepted Pieter's hand. "You act just like a little old grannie woman, you know that?"

"Yeah, vell maybe I do, but you do like I say or else."

Willie smiled at their playfulness and then put on his heavy coat. He still had to see about the horses.

On his way to the stable, he looked at the sky. "I wonder if it'll ever be warm again." Heavy clouds promised more snow. He looked forward to the warm spring weather that would melt the snow and thaw the rivers. Life would be much easier. He sighed. The fighting would pick up, too, with warmer weather. The Colonial army was pitifully clothed, and many had no boots. In the Mohawk Valley of New York Province where Willie lived, the fighting was mostly looting, pillaging and harassing. But with warm weather, new troops would be organized on both sides and a thawed river meant transporting supplies.

He smiled as he heard his horse nicker. He opened the heavy door to the stable. "Hey, Running Wind, you black devil."

He stroked the big stallion's mane and face. "You like this petting, don't you?"

The other two horses in their stalls wanted to be petted, too. "All right, Cannonball and Nellie, I'll rub you a bit."

He talked to the horses a few minutes more before bolting the door behind him.

A light snow had begun to fall. Again Willie sighed as he hugged his coat around him and hurried toward the warm cabin.

Willie woke with a start. His father was moaning. He rushed down the ladder from his loft room to his father's side and felt his forehead. It was burning hot. "Vater, you all right?"

In the dim firelight, Willie watched Karl's tortured face. He mumbled in Dutch: "Veel moeite, Willie." His words meant he was in much pain.

Continuing in a hoarse whisper, he tried to be casual, "Guess that bear grease and pitch weren't strong enough medicine, or I just lost too much blood. Hurts like the devil itself."

Willie lit a candle and looked at the swollen arm. He loosened the bandage and looked at the ugly wound. He applied more bear grease and pitch, wrinkling his nose at the smell.

Karl made a face, too. "Smells bad, don't it?"

"Sure does. Maybe we ain't giving it enough time to do its job."

"Maybe."

Willie felt fear creeping in. "I need to bring that fever down."

"Maybe it'll wear itself out."

"I'll make some catnip tea."

Karl groaned as Willie put more wood on the fire and pulled the iron kettle near. While the water heated, he took down the cloth bag with the herbs tied neatly inside. There was boneset root, catnip and prickly ash bark, all Indian remedies for fever and other ailments. Once more Willie was glad his mother had taught him so many of her ways, and especially how to identify and gather nature's medicines.

After helping his father get most of the tea down, Willie covered him and put cloths on his forehead. Karl kept kicking at the covers, but Willie patiently put them back. He wanted him to sweat. It wasn't long before beads of perspiration formed on Karl's forehead.

Willie glanced at the drawn curtain that separated them from the area where his grandfather slept. No need to wake him. Willie guessed it was a blessing at times to be hard of hearing.

Willie thought about his Dutch grandfather. The old man had great cause to rebel at the British stranglehold attempt. Pieter Krol had told the boy many times how he had saved for years to buy a boat ticket so that he and his young bride could come to America.

Willie never knew his grandmother. His father told him she had literally worn herself out from hard work and worry. Like many of the Dutch settlers, Pieter and his wife had lived in Albany. There he had worked and saved until he was able to buy land from a patroon.* The Krols, with their son, Karl, had built a sturdy cabin and farmed the virgin soil. To Pieter Krol, land was a sacred thing worth fighting for—dying for, if necessary.

The Dutch farmer had fought in the French and Indian War for the right to be free. Now the British dared their hand at taking away his freedom.

Willie listened to the soft snoring of the old man, no longer able to fight. He felt very sorry for his grandfather.

With one hand on his father's shoulder, Willie dozed off.

He woke with a start to see Karl looking at him in the dim light. "You better, Vater?" the boy asked, still worried.

"Fever broke, thanks to my doctor son."

"Wasn't nothin'."

"Wasn't, huh? Your mother always said you had a way with healing. Remember the baby deer you found caught under that log? You nursed it back to health and turned it loose when it was big enough to take care of itself."

Willie remembered. "Wonder what happened to him."

---

*patroon—head of a large manor or estate

Karl shrugged. "Probably a great grandfather many times over."

They chuckled at their silliness. Willie felt a surge of relief; his father was going to be all right.

Karl sniffed and flexed his good shoulder. "Your mother and I always felt that this talent you have ought to be put to good use. Maybe someday you can study to be a doctor."

Willie remembered his mother telling him that he would one day be a doctor, but he hadn't thought of it much since she died. "I guess I'd like that, Father."

Karl patted his son's knee. "We'll keep it heavy on our minds."

Willie stood up and stretched. "What about that errand you were going to do? Want me to go in your stead?"

Karl did not answer at once, but looked deep into his son's face. "You could do it, but I'd worry about you."

Willie shook his head. "I'd be extra careful." He felt his heart beating fast in anticipation.

Karl bit his bottom lip in thought, and then said, "Think you can ride to Albany and get a message to General Schuyler?"

The boy's eyes widened. "Yes, sir, I can."

He had never been to Albany alone. Suddenly, he felt very grown-up. "Yes, sir, I sure can do it," he repeated.

Karl shifted in bed, moving his injured arm carefully. "All right, son. Listen well: You are to tell the general that Colonel Henry Knox left Fort Ticonderoga in January with fifty-nine pieces of artillery on slides pulled by oxen. He's making his way to Boston where the Colonials are desperate for artillery. When he gets it there, it'll end the siege."

Willie nodded his understanding.

Karl continued. "Tell the general to have fresh oxen, supplies and an escort ready to go on with the colonel to Boston."

Willie nodded again.

"Now repeat the message to me, son."

Willie swallowed, then repeated the message almost word for word. "That Colonel Knox must be one tough fellow," he remarked.

Karl nodded. "Gutsy all right. Of course, winter's the best time to do something like that what with the lakes and rivers frozen. And too, not so much interference from the enemy in the bitter cold."

Willie nodded. "He's sure to make history with that oxen train."

Karl agreed, but asked, *"Sure* you can do it?"

Willie straightened his shoulders. He looked taller. "You bet."

Karl smiled. "You know I'm mighty proud to have you for a son?"

"No prouder than I am to have you for my father."

Karl squeezed his son's arm. A shiver raced over the boy and he shrugged it off, but not before his father saw. "Sure you're all right?"

"Yes, just excited, I guess."

"Some excitement is good. Keeps you alert—but don't let it get out of hand."

Willie shook his head. "No, sir, I won't."

"You'll have to leave at first light. Try to get a little rest."

Willie knew he couldn't sleep, but he would lie down. As he started to his ladder, his father added, "Better take food with you. It'll be a day's ride or more."

Willie nodded and climbed up to his loft bed.

CHAPTER TWO

To Albany

Running Wind must have known how important their journey was—he was behaving just like a trained cavalry horse.

Willie repeated to himself his father's instructions: First, travel southeast toward the Hudson River. The pale winter sun reluctantly marked his way, and the cold wind chilled him right through his beaver pelt coat. He patted the note inside his deerskin shirt and remembered his father's words: "Better write you a note of introduction. He might not believe my Indian son."

Willie bit his lip. He knew it was true—they might not believe him. He was to find someone in command and not tell anyone else that he had a message. Since Albany was one-third loyalist, it might be hard to tell who could be trusted.

He sighed and fought at the doubt—and fear—that tried to creep inside him. "We gonna take a rest, Running Wind; mostly for you, 'cause you're doing all the work."

He smiled as he remembered his grandfather's words: "You ought to ride with a saddle like a white man. You'd have better control of your mount and wouldn't get so tired." But he liked riding bareback. The blanket was enough. His horse was freer and so was he. Besides, Running Wind would never accept a saddle.

He let his mind drift to Henry Knox and pictured the great train of oxen and sleds carrying the artillery to Boston. What a brave man Knox must be to struggle against the weather and the mountains with a forty-two sled ox train. He whistled under his breath. Fort Ticonderoga was a long, long way from Boston and the train would have to go over Indian trails and through a lot of deep snow in places. In his young mind he pictured the oxen laboring to get onto the frozen lakes and rivers where the going would be much easier.

Compared to Colonel Knox's mission, Willie's seemed small. That thought gave him courage to continue. He nudged his stallion lightly to hurry along. He would soon be out of the mountains and into the valley.

The timid sun was about to sink behind the mountain, and he began looking for a place to spend the night. The boy's sharp eyes scanned the area for an overhang or a cave.

He felt his stomach growl. Supper was the pemmican in his shoulder bag. It was nothing more than dried strips of meat, with a few berries and fat pounded in, but it would stave off hunger.

The boy spied a cave large enough for him and his horse. "At least we'll be warm inside the cave. It's bad enough to be hungry, but worse to be cold."

Willie was filled with disappointment at the short distance he had been able to travel in the heavy snow. Then he thought of his mother's words to him in times such as this. "Tomorrow will be better, my son." He nodded to himself. He knew that it would.

The morning dawned brightly, and the world too was freshly white with the snow that had fallen during the night. Willie led his mount out from the cave and said, "It's cold as blue blazes, but at least it's not snowing. The wind is still, too." He shivered.

A fire was out of the question. He ate the rest of the pemmican and pulled out the dried fodder he had brought for his horse. "Maybe we can find some grain for you in Albany."

After an hour or so of riding, he was still in the Mohawk Valley. Scanning the vast horizon, Willie thought of the Mohawk Indians, considered by many to be the most powerful nation of the League of Iroquois; its warriors were the most feared.

The boy let his mind go back to the time he had sat at his mother's knee and she had told him of the Iroquois Confederacy. The Indians treasure the story of a very peaceful Mohawk and his disciple, Hiawatha, who persuaded all the tribes to join together and put an end to their quarrels, living as good neighbors, according to certain laws and rules. United in that way, the tribes became strong and famous—successful in everything they did. The legend said that Hiawatha, that ancient Chieftain of the Mohawks, gave special powers to his people to protect them from evil forces. He taught them how to grow food and practice medicine and sail ships.

Willie said aloud to his horse, "Boy, he was really something, that Hiawatha, wasn't he?" The boy knew that most of the stories were not entirely true, but it was pleasant to think about and to pretend that it was all exactly as it had been told for the past two hundred years.

Willie continued to ride through the big valley. Many years ago, the door to the West had been guarded by the Seneca, his mother's people; the door to the East had been guarded by the Mohawk; while in the center of the region, the Onondagas served as keepers of the fires.

Looking at the magnificent land all around him, Willie sighed. The tribes of the League of Six Nations were no longer united; all had chosen to be loyal to the British except the Oneida and Tuscarora who stayed with the Colonists.

Near the Mohawk River now, Willie moved more carefully. He could see and smell distant campfire smoke. Was it from Tory fires? It could be. Most of the colonists had gone on to Albany for protection, burning their fields and houses before leaving.

The boy decided to stay as close to the river as possible, using the wooded banks for cover. He picked his way through the tall timber and suddenly a clearing was before him. It was once the site of a homestead. Now it was burned out; the smell of smoky timbers filled his nostrils.

The boy rode around the clearing a few minutes and as he turned back toward the riverbank, two horsemen seemed to appear from nowhere. Should he run or stay? His heart picked up speed. He would stay and try and talk his way out of this.

The motley pair rode up next to him. They were young, and their clothes were ragged and dirty. Willie quickly decided they were Tories.

One spoke as he pulled up his nag. "Well, what have we here? an Injun? Or is it a white young'un?"

Willie stared coldly into the man's bloodshot eyes.

The other, dressed in an ill-fitting coat, said gruffly, "What you doing and where you goin'? You just a kid, ain't you?"

"Almost fifteen," he said quietly through clenched teeth.

"Well, well, he speaks the King's English, and quite well."

"You a Wyandot?" the other stranger asked.

They wouldn't know the difference between tribes, so Willie nodded. "I'm hunting fresh meat."

"That a fact? Where's your gun?"

The boy swallowed. "I use my knife." With one hand, he pulled his coat aside to show the knife at his side.

"Slip up on 'em, do you?"

Willie nodded.

The dirtier of the two scratched his stubbled chin and dismounted. He walked around Willie. "Don't look like no Wyandot to me. More like a Mohawk or maybe an Oneida?"

The one still mounted smiled, revealing holes where teeth had been. "Mighty fine stallion. What'll you trade for him?"

Willie shook his head. The one on the ground pointed at his knapsack. "Got anything of value in there?"

Once more, Willie shook his head and tensed himself for flight. He realized that Running Wind, who was prancing nervously, could sense his feelings.

"How come you wearin' white man's clothes?" the man continued. "And how'd you learn to speak such good English which you now refuse to use?"

The mounted one said, "Seems a mite strange, don't it? Let's take him to camp and let *them* question him. Might be a spy."

As quick as a flash, Willie swung his foot and shoved as hard as he could. The Tory, caught off guard, fell off his horse and on top of his friend. Willie nudged his mount and galloped away from them. They yelled and quickly prepared to come after him. One fired a shot. Willie wasn't afraid of being caught—there wasn't a horse in the entire New York Colony that could outrun his—he was afraid that the shot might attract men from the encampment over the next rise.

Instinct told him to head back for the mountains, but his judgment said to continue to Albany.

The boy's long hair flew in the cold wind. His floppy hat threatened to leave his head at any second. Willie saw a knoll ahead and raced for it, looking back only once to see if the Tories were still after him. He could not see them.

Looking from right to left, Willie frantically thought what he should do. As he topped the knoll, the frozen Mohawk River lay below. He listened carefully. The Tories were not coming. He breathed a sigh of relief and patted Running Wind's neck. "You're just too fast for 'em."

Willie looked down at the river. As always, it was snaking its way toward Albany. It would be easier for him and the stallion to walk across it. He dismounted.

Once across, the boy looked all around him before mounting and continuing on his way. He squinted into the sun and noticed a lone rider. The boy sighed. What now? He rode slowly, giving the rider time to catch up with him.

The tall rider wore a green stocking cap. He had on clean deerskin pants and a bearskin coat. He was a bony sort, but graceful, and he sat very straight in his saddle.

"Morning."

Willie nodded, not sure if he should speak or not.

"Can't you talk, boy? Half Indian, aren't you? Seneca, maybe?"

Willie could not remember ever having been recognized as a Seneca. "Yes."

The rider blinked and said freely, "Who's your folks?"

Willie knew that if he told this stranger who he was, he would be revealing whether he was for the British or the Colonials. He hesitated. Even his few short years on earth had taught him when and when not to trust. Yet he decided that he liked this slow speaking man. Willie looked straight into the stranger's eyes: "If you're asking to learn if I'm for the British or the Colonials, it's the Colonials."

A slow smile spread over the homely face. "Somehow, I knew. You just look like a young man with a cause."

Willie let those remarks sink in and then said, "I'm Willie Krol and my father is Karl Krol. He's in the New York Militia, Thompson's outfit."

As quick as a flash, Willie swung his foot and shoved as hard as he could. The Tory, caught off guard, fell off his horse and on top of his friend. Willie nudged his mount and galloped away from them.

The rider laughed aloud. "I know old Karl well. We did some scoutin' awhile back."

Willie smiled, "And what's your name?"

The man held out his hand, and Willie shook it firmly. "I'm Horace Cuyler."

"Why, I've heard my father speak of you. Said you are one gutsy fellow."

Horace smiled. "Karl's no slouch himself."

Relief spilled over the boy. He had found a friend of his father's. "My father was hurt a couple of days ago," Willie confided. "I'm going to Albany in his stead with a message for General Schuyler."

Horace scratched his head through the wool cap. "Was he hurt bad?"

"No, a flesh wound. It'll be good enough in a few days, but he didn't need to ride that far right now."

Horace nodded. "Ever been to Albany?"

"Once with my folks—to see my father's sister, Aunt Gladys. She's kind of snobbish, best I remember."

"Well, Willie, this war's taken a lot of snobbery out of folks. Something called humility has crept in its place. The city's changed a lot in the past year or so. Folks are moving in there from the country for protection. Right crowded there now."

"I sure don't plan staying any longer than it takes to get my message to the general. Got to find him first, though."

"I'll show you."

"I'd be obliged, sir."

"We best speed up these horses a mite. Albany's no more than an hour away."

They rode in silence awhile. Willie wondered why Cuyler didn't ask him what the message was, but supposed he just wasn't the kind of fellow to ask something like that.

Horace sniffed and said, "You a brave young man to be doing this for your country."

"Well, I don't feel brave enough. Just something that has to be done."

"How old are you?"

"Almost fifteen."

"So your mother is Seneca Indian?"

"Yes, sir, but she's dead. Died almost three years ago from a fever. She was the chief's daughter. After they were married, my father brought her back from near the great lake to the west of here."

"You don't say? Well, I know she was a nice person to have loved old Karl and to have a son like you."

Willie was a little embarrassed, but deep inside he felt warmed by those words.

Suddenly, Willie found himself telling Horace about the Tories chasing him and firing the gun.

"I heard the shot," Horace remarked. "Just figured it was somebody hunting game."

"I was scared, I tell you. I wasn't afraid of being caught, 'cause no horse alive can outrun mine, but I *was* afraid of being shot and not getting my message to the general."

"I can understand that."

Still, Horace did not ask about the message. Willie almost wished he would; he would have liked to share it with him. The boy shivered visibly and Horace asked, "Are you all right?"

"Just a little cold and a whole lot worried."

Horace pulled his cap down to better cover his own big ears. "A man, let alone a boy, would be a fool not to ever admit he was scared during a war."

Somehow the statement was calming, though Willie couldn't explain why. Who was this man who could make him feel twice his age? It was almost frightening to the boy.

"How'd you learn to speak such good English?" Horace asked.

Willie smiled. "Guess my father and grandfather mostly. But I spent a year in my mother's village learning her ways. My father thought it would be good. The missionaries came and taught my mother and me to read and write."

Horace shook his head. "Well, you seem to have some mighty fine education."

Willie scanned the horizon, still thinking of his mother. "She and my father wanted me to study medicine when I get old enough. They both thought I had a natural talent."

Horace sighed and lifted his bushy eyebrows. "Well, Albany is about the best place I can think of to learn medicine. Seems any and everybody that knows anything about doctoring has gathered in Albany."

Willie looked surprised. "I didn't know that."

"Yep. Well, the entire city is kind of like a quartermaster store and supply depot for soldiers fighting on the frontier. So surely there needs to be folks capable of doctoring." He smiled to himself and then said, "However, the Common Council in Albany claims there's only two methods for combating disease and sickness. One, they said, is prayer and fasting, and the other is quarantine." He laughed aloud.

Willie did not understand what was funny, but laughed with his new friend anyway.

The two soon topped a knoll and the city of Albany lay before them. Willie gasped. "It's big!"

A lazy smile crossed Horace's face. "You should see New York City, Boston and Philadelphia. They make Albany look like a hamlet."

"You been to all those places?"

"Yep. But ain't no big thing. Didn't especially like 'em and came back here to the Mohawk and Hudson Valley."

Willie asked, "Where do you live?"

Horace smiled. "Well, I have a place in Tryon County near Fort Stanwix." He sighed. "Then I have another place in Albany where I hang my hat."

Willie whistled softly, "Two places?"

"Neither one of 'em is much to brag about. The place in Tryon County has a lot of acres, but since the war started, everybody up there seems to sympathize with the British, so I been spending most of my time here. Just a lean-to on the west side of town. I'll go back to Tryon County soon, though. I understand old Nicholas Herkimer is working hard to raise a big force of New York militiamen against Sir John Johnson."

When Willie looked at him questioningly, Horace explained. "Herkimer is a brigadier general of the New York militia. General Schuyler has ordered him to raid Johnson Hall. Say, did you ever hear of Sir *William* Johnson?"

Willie nodded. "Yes, my grandfather told me all about how he had gotten the Indians to be loyal to the British, that he had died before the war started, and that he had been quite a character."

Horace smirked. "I'll say. It's because of him that the Six Nations are for the British, except for the Oneida and Tuscarora of course. His son John is rowdier than William ever was; a cruel fellow. He's been doing some bad things to the folks around Fort Stanwix, and Herkimer intends to make him pay."

"That Herkimer fellow must be something," Willie commented as they crossed a stream.

"He is. Nearly fifty—black hair and snapping dark eyes. He's a rugged, square-built German. Owns a lot of acreage around there."

Willie laughed. "Well, if Herkimer is that tough, Mr. Johnson better watch his step."

Horace smiled. "I'll be going there too, as soon as I finish my business in Albany."

Willie wondered what that business was but dared not ask.

"Must be a thousand houses here," Willie remarked as the two riders made their way into the city.

"Last count, Willie, was something like 500 dwelling houses, not counting stores and outhouses."

Willie had never seen so many people in his life, either. Women screamed at small children from windows. A boy herded a drove of squealing pigs across the rutted street. An old man shoveled manure onto a low sled behind an ox. The smell of the fresh manure and wood smoke made Willie's stomach twitch.

Horace saw him swallow. "Nothing's all good, is it?"

They made their way through the crowded street. Willie hoped that they would soon get where they were going.

The two turned down a tree-lined street, not so well traveled, and passed through the gate of an old fort. The gate had almost rotted with age.

Horace said, "The old fort's about gone. It was a good one during the French and Indian War. There's talk about fixin' it up. Seems to me they ought to either fix it up or build a new one in these times of war."

Willie nodded and pointed down the hill at the Dutch Reformed Church on Broadway. "What's that big church?"

"That's the Dutch church. They had to build it bigger in 1715 to accommodate all those holy Dutchmen." He grinned at Willie.

"Are there lots of churches here?"

"I'll say. Something close to ten churches. Lutheran, Catholic, Anglican, Presbyterian and maybe a Methodist. Some of them meet in homes, though—don't have a church building."

Willie sighed. "I never been to a real church. We don't have one in our valley."

"I know, I know. Well, you know what they say, 'Religion starts in the heart.'" Horace pounded his heart lightly and continued. "All them pretty buildings ain't worth nothing if the heart ain't right."

Willie smiled. "That's the way the Senecas believe, too."

Horace nodded. "Church is good, no bones about it, but it's not enough by itself."

Horace sniffed as they rode around a small cart. "Ever hear of Lord Howe?"

Willie shook his head.

"Old Lord Howe was a real friend of the colonists during the French and Indian War. He took a bullet at the Battle of Ticonderoga in 1758. Schuyler thought enough of him to bring his remains back to Albany." Horace pointed back to the Anglican Church. "They buried him under his church back there."

"That seems a nice thing to do."

"Yep, it was. Well, son, we about waded through. I live right over there in that house on the corner. When you finish, come back here. I'll see if I can find something for us to eat and some grain for your mount. Right now, though, I'm going to look for a newspaper—if the *Gazette's* still printing." He pointed a long finger. "You just keep going on down this street all the way to the end. That's where you'll find the camp and General Schuyler's place. Ask; they'll show you."

Willie nodded and took a good look at the house in order to remember it. "Thanks so much, Horace. See you soon."

The boy rode along, looking around him all the while. The city seemed better here. Trees grew along the streets and some of the houses were quite nice. He was filled with the sights, sounds and smells of the city. Bystanders and soldiers were staring at him, an Indian boy on a fine black stallion, riding bareback and dressed in white man's clothes. Not much time had passed before a soldier said sarcastically, "Hey, Injun, want to trade that hoss? I got some pretty beads I'll swap you."

Willie ignored him. He had learned long ago that useless words babbled forth from the mouths of fools. They were not worthy of his attention.

Finally, he came to the end of the street. A span of army tents and frame buildings covered a big area. The boy saw a rather large building with a flag waving on top. He decided to try there.

A young soldier stood near the door. Willie dismounted and walked toward him with straight shoulders. His heart had picked up a little speed in anticipation of this, the most important part of his trip. Courteously, he said, "I'm looking for General Schuyler."

The soldier burst into laughter. "So's a lot of folks a heap more important than you. State your business, Halfbreed."

The cruel words did not phase him outwardly, but inside Willie wanted to smash that jeering face. Just as suddenly, though, his mother's calm words came to mind, "People who say mean things are either ignorant or angry with themselves. Even wishful revenge is wrong and will change nothing."

He sighed. "I have business with the general or someone under his command."

The soldier shifted his musket to rest it near his foot. "I'm under his command. We all under his command; what do you want?" Other soldiers standing around joined in with the jeering.

Willie fought at the anger rising slowly in his throat. "I have no time for your games."

More laughter. "An educated injun. Hear how pretty he talks."

Suddenly, the door swung open, and the soldiers jerked to attention.

Willie looked into the face of the most distinguished person he had ever seen. The man's tailored uniform, decorated with many beautiful buttons, was spotless. He wore a powdered wig with a large curl at the bottom. Though tall and lanky, he was powerfully built. His brown eyes looked deep into Willie's eyes, then at the soldiers standing about. "What's all this noise about?"

The soldier with the musket said quickly, "This injun wants to see you, sir."

The general looked once more into Willie's face and, raising an eyebrow, asked, "Why?"

"I have a message, sir."

The general heaved a sigh. "Very well. Come in quickly. I have much to do."

Willie hurried inside and shut the door. He worked his eyes to adjust them to the dimly-lit room. It was warm, but a little shiver of gratitude ran over him.

The general faced Willie and wrung his smooth hands slowly. "All right, young man, what is it?" he sighed. "And sit down."

Willie turned and sat on a rough stool. He glanced at a silver tray on the table. It held a plate of half-eaten food.

"I'm sorry I disturbed your meal."

The general glanced at the tray. "I'm all finished. Can't get decent food anymore."

Willie's mouth watered for the food that the general had left on the plate. He swallowed, then spoke. "My father is Karl Krol. He's with the New York Militia, Thompson's outfit. He was slightly injured day before yesterday in a fight with the Tories. I'm here in his stead." He quickly handed him his father's note.

The general read quickly, then nodded. "Very well, what's the message?"

Willie swallowed and then told General Schuyler about Knox and the artillery.

Schuyler folded his arms, and when he was sure Willie was finished, said almost sadly, "I knew he had orders to do this from Washington himself, but I never thought he'd be able to pull it off, what with the disastrous failure of the Canadian invasion." He sighed and rubbed his chin. "Knox wrote me in December and asked for 500 fathom of three-inch rope to tie the cannon onto sleds." He shook his head once more. "I sent him the rope, never thinking for a moment he'd be able to do it."

Willie saw what he thought was a smile playing at the corners of the general's mouth.

"It's a foolish stunt, but I can't help but admire the spunky fellow."

Willie smiled. "Yes, sir. Me too, sir. From Lake George, they'll be traveling the old military road here to Albany..."

The general finished his sentence, "...then across the frozen Hudson, through the Berkshires to Cambridge where they'll more than likely be able to end the Boston occupation."

The general seemed almost in a trance as he spoke. Willie figured that Schuyler probably wished *he* was with that ox train. The boy had heard that General Schuyler was not in good health and suffered with gout, but it was obvious that the veteran Dutch soldier had seen a lot in his lifetime. General Schuyler sipped from a tiny cup. "I'll do all I can. A quartermaster general with not enough supplies for his own can do little for a foolhardy colonel on a foolhardy mission. I'll probably be able to round up what he needs. I'm glad you brought me the message."

Willie felt good and straightened his shoulders. "Thank you, sir."

It seemed the general had not heard the boy. Schuyler stared down at a map and muttered, "Never thought a bookseller from Boston would be commissioned a colonel of artillery the way Knox was."

"Yes, sir. Father says he's a man of great strength and character like you, sir."

The general looked over his spectacles at the boy. "Thank you, young man." He looked more closely at the big map before him. "By your father's calculations, where do you suppose Knox is by now?"

Willie stretched to try and see the map.

"Get up and come here," the man said impatiently. "Show me where you think they are."

Willie walked quickly to the general's chair and peered down at the map. He at once picked out the Hudson and Mohawk and then leaned down to pinpoint the ox train's probable location. "Father said they were at Fort Miller, right about here, on Tuesday."

The general nodded. "That means he's making about ten miles a day."

"And more on good days."

The general looked into Willie's face and seemed to really notice him. "How old are you, Willie?"

"Fifteen." He was tired of saying *almost* fifteen.

"Your mother Indian?"

"Seneca. My father's Dutch."

"Sorry you're not old enough to be in my army. You're all right."

There was no special emotion in his voice—just a plain statement which Willie wasn't sure how to answer. "Father says we have to do what we can, no matter our age."

"Your father's right."

"Yes, sir."

"Go back and tell him I'll be expecting Knox and his circus." He reached out and shook Willie's hand firmly. "Thank you for coming, young man."

Willie nodded and thought he saw a hint of a smile, but wasn't sure. Maybe he just wanted it to be there.

The general then pushed some newspapers to one side to make room for another map. Willie stood at the door and said, "Sir? Are you finished with any of those newspapers?"

The general glanced at the papers and then up at the Indian lad. "You can read, too?"

"Yes, sir."

The general bundled up several papers and thrust them at the boy. "Take them. They're old, but it's news anyway."

"Thank you, sir." Willie folded them together and quickly stuffed them inside his coat.

The general, again concentrating on his work, did not look up as Willie quietly closed the door behind him.

The cold wind snatched at the boy's hat. He pulled it down tightly with both hands. Mounting his horse, he headed away from the camp, neither looking at the soldiers standing nearby nor listening to their hateful remarks.

There was no one at Horace's house. The boy waited a few minutes in the cold wind and decided that something must have detained the man elsewhere, so Willie headed out of town.

Running Wind tucked his head at the biting wind, and Willie did the same. His stomach growled with hunger. He thought of the uneaten food on the general's plate, but his main concern at this point was for his horse.

He planned to stop at the Shaker Community a few miles out from town. He and Horace had passed it on the way into Albany. Willie had heard of Mother Ann Lee who had come from Manchester, England and founded this community near Watervliet. He didn't know anything about the Shakers' beliefs, but he did know that they were kind and charitable people who would share their food with him and give him grain for his horse if they had it.

Willie sat on the floor with the newspapers spread before him. His father sat in a chair nearby with some of the papers on his lap.

"I'm really proud of you, Willie. You did a powerful good job on your mission."

"Thank you." He looked down, a bit embarrassed as always at compliments.

"Maybe I'll take you scoutin' sometimes."

The boy brightened. "That would be something."

Grandfather looked over his spectacles. "You best not, Karl. He's but a boy and all we got."

Willie warmed at his grandfather's words, but wished that old Pieter would think of him as more than a boy.

Karl shifted in his chair, careful not to hurt his injured arm. "He's a boy in years, but in other ways, he's full grown."

Willie shook his head and looked back at the newspapers. "Nothing in these papers we didn't already know."

Karl said, "They're about three months old. Even before the attempt to take Quebec, and Montgomery's death."

The boy had already told his father about Horace, but had failed to tell him about Herkimer's getting troops lined up. Willie grinned. "I got some news newer than this old paper."

Grandfather and Karl looked quickly at him. Karl said, "What's that?"

Willie leaned back against the wall near the fireplace and told them about Schuyler's orders to muster 3,000 troops and that Horace was going to be a part of it all.

Karl nodded, "He would. That devil likes to go ahuntin' trouble. But if I know him, he'll come back if he has to sit in one spot very long waiting for trouble *or* battle to start."

Willie raised himself up and put on his coat and gloves. "I'm going to split some wood."

Karl and Pieter nodded as he picked up the ax and opened the heavy door. Willie felt safe in the haven of his valley. His stomach was full from the game stew and he felt loved.

As he chopped away at the wood, he wondered how long the good feeling would last. He knew that many would have to die before the war would end. The thought saddened and frightened him. Would those he loved be among the dead?

He split a big pile of wood and then walked slowly to the grove of white birch to visit his mother's grave. He would pour out his heart to her—she always listened.

CHAPTER THREE

In Early Spring—1777

Willie stepped carefully through the deep snow. He walked backward a few steps, watching his snowshoe tracks as he went. Suddenly, he stopped and yelled to the mountains around him: "Hurry up, Spring! I'm tired of being cold!" The boy laughed as his echo bounced across the mountains. Although it was late March, the day was still bitter cold. A sharp wind eased through Willie's heavy coat.

He turned and headed toward home, hoisting the two big snowshoe rabbits to his other shoulder. He'd tracked them quite a distance before finding the snow covered briar patch where they had gone. Willie had placed a snare at both openings. Then he had beaten on top of the briars with a heavy stick. A rabbit had come out from each opening, falling into the carefully placed snares. Mercifully, Willie had broken their necks. Now, they would go into the stew pot for another good meal.

Willie sniffed and wondered if there were enough flour to make bread to go with the fresh stew. The wheat and maize crops had been scanty. There was little time for proper farming with a war going on. And what a war!

More had happened than Willie cared to remember: The Continental Congress couldn't make up its mind who would be in charge of the northern command, General Schuyler or the dowdy Horatio Gates who would not take a chance, no matter what. Schuyler was not a fighting field commander, but an excellent organizer. He was outstanding in getting things done, but left the actual field battle to other men, men like Benedict Arnold. Willie sighed. What a brave man Benedict Arnold was.

The past summer, Arnold, General Schuyler, Gates and others had met at Crown Point, deciding to build a navy to stop the British from coming down Lake Champlain. Willie sighed as he thought of the report of that battle.

Benedict Arnold had taken the navy ships and sailed to meet the British. The Tory ships made the American navy look puny. But with the ships so quickly built and the three they had captured from the British a year earlier, Arnold had outsmarted the British at the Battle of Valcour Island on Lake Champlain. Even though the British had won the battle, Benedict Arnold had delayed them to the point that they could not go on to Ticonderoga to take it over, but were forced back to Canada until the following spring.

The "victory" Arnold had won was in delaying the British for almost a full year. Willie smiled. It was said that "Granny" Gates would never have fought such a daring battle. He was ever too cautious.

Since Karl Krol was in the militia, he was informed about all that was happening, and he kept his son informed, too. Willie was glad. The Colonials were well aware that a certain "Gentleman Johnny Burgoyne" was in Canada, waiting for the rivers to thaw so that he could come and take care of the "rebellious Americans." Willie wondered if Burgoyne knew of the preparations the Americans were making for his debut.

The boy hastened his steps. The pale sun told him it would be dark in a couple of hours.

He glanced down and saw fresh deer tracks. His mind left the cruel war. His father had promised they would go hunting for deer tomorrow. He would get to use his bow and arrow.

His mother's tribe had hunted deer differently. The men stalked the animals to the edge of the cliff and frightened them over the edge, where the women waited to dress the meat. The boy knew of some tribes in the Lake George area who did this along a mountain ledge called, appropriately enough, "Deer Leap."

Even with his Indian blood and the teaching of a tough father and grandfather, this method seemed cruel to Willie. He thought the silent and almost painless arrow by far the better way to hunt meat.

He was glad to see the familiar cabin come into view. His legs and feet were tired from walking in the snow.

He tossed the rabbits on the porch and peeled off his snowshoes and gloves. "Wet gloves are like no gloves." He rubbed his cold hands together to get the circulation going.

Grandfather opened the door. "Got two good ones, huh?"

Willie nodded and smiled. "They were hard to find; must have known the Krols were rabbit hungry."

The old man chuckled. "You cold as ice, you are. Come inside and varm up before you skin 'em."

"I'd rather get it done and then warm up. It wouldn't be the same knowing I had to come right back out and do the job."

Grandfather nodded. "You got it all figured out, ain't you?"

Willie smiled his reply. He made a quick slit with his knife and began skinning his catch.

It didn't take long for Gramps to get the stew bubbling merrily in the big pot. Willie sat before the crackling fire absorbing its warmth and enjoying the aroma from the pot. His grandfather had placed the cut meat, herbs and a little of the precious salt in the pot. Willie's stomach growled in anticipation of the good food.

Gramps sat in the big rocker he had built and puffed at his briar pipe. "Karl vent to swap some pelts for flour at the fort."

Willie nodded. "Those were really nice pelts." His mind wandered back to the day they had run the traps on Buster Kill, a creek too swift to freeze over. There had been three big mink, an otter and a beaver. "I wanted to go with him, but he thought I ought to hunt the rabbits."

"Everyone's gotta do his part."

Willie nodded. He listened. "Someone's coming!"

Suddenly, he heard his father's booming voice. "Willie! Vater! Come quickly!"

They hurried out to see what all the commotion was about. Karl rode fast into the yard. Someone was riding behind him.

"Come help, son."

Willie rushed to Karl's side and helped the rider from the horse. He peered into the face of a very frightened Indian girl. She went limp in his arms. He knew she was almost frozen.

Grandfather watched. "Vere'd you find her, Karl?"

Karl dismounted and handed the flour to his father. "Wandering near the river. She speaks a little English. I made out that her tribe had kicked her out." Karl reached out toward Willie and took the girl in his arms. "Don't know why, though," he muttered as he carried her inside.

Willie looked into her face. Her tortured eyes saddened him. She reminded him of the little deer he had once found. Her look tugged at his heart now as the deer's look had then.

Karl stood the girl down gently and led her to a low stool near the fire. She mumbled something over and over.

He listened. "Someone's coming!"
Suddenly he heard his father's booming voice. "Willie! Vater! Come quickly!"

Willie helped her off with the bearskin coat, but she hugged still another blanket close.

He said to her, "Gayah-da-sey." It meant that they were her friends.

He saw her swallow. Tears began to fill her eyes. He repeated the friendly words again.

Karl said, "Warm some cloths before the fire and wrap her hands and feet. It'll help get her blood stirring."

Willie brought cloths from the chest and warmed them.

Grandfather said, "Vich tribe, you reckon?"

"Maybe Oneida," Karl said with a shrug. "She ran from me when I called to her, then collapsed in the snow. Don't look a day over sixteen."

The girl looked at Willie. He thought he saw a sad little smile cross her face and then disappear. He wiped the tears from her cheeks with a warm cloth and said softly, "Gayah-da-sey."

He pointed to the pot. "Eat?"

Her black eyes widened and she nodded.

Pieter said, "That's one thing everybody understands—eat."

Karl smiled and nodded.

Willie brought a bowl and wooden spoon and held it while Grandfather dipped it full of the thick rabbit stew. His mouth watered as he carried it to her. She began eating quickly, and her dark eyes darted from one to the other.

Karl said, "How about us joining her? I'm starved."

Willie was sure glad his father made that suggestion.

After supper, they sat around the table and talked. The Indian girl sat looking out the window.

Karl caught her eye and motioned for her to come sit down with them. As she turned, the blanket fell and she grabbed it, but not before Karl saw. "She's with child," he said softly.

Pieter shook his head sadly. "Probably vy they kicked her out."

Willie tried not to stare at her. A strange feeling came over him. He had seen women with child, but he felt silly thinking her a woman since she was probably not much more than his age.

Karl said gently, "Papoose?"

The girl placed her hand on her stomach and smiled for the first time.

Pieter puffed on a cold pipe. "That's all ve need—a pregnant squaw."

Willie swallowed hard. "Will the baby be born soon?"

Karl sighed. "Very soon, I'd say."

Willie wasn't sure how he should feel about all this.

Karl asked in his faltering Indian dialect, "Father? Who's baby's father?"

A frantic look crossed the girl's face. Tears filled her eyes once more. She said simply, "Soldier."

Karl shook his head. "She was probably forced."

Willie's eyes darted from one to the other. He knew about babies being born. Everyone who lived on a farm knew from seeing animals bearing their young. But his mind could not grasp the idea of *force*.

Grandfather, as though reading his mind, said gently, "This is a cruel vorld at times. Everybody on earth ain't decent."

"She's so pitiful, Gramps." He turned to his father and searched his face for a clue as to how he should feel about all this. There was none. It was a decision he must make for himself.

Karl walked to the window and watched the falling snow. "Maybe the snow will let up tomorrow. I'll figure out what to do about this."

Pieter sniffed. "Vell, you askin' for trouble to keep her here."

Karl sighed. "We'll do what we have to do."

Willie asked the young maiden her name.

"Little Fawn."

He smiled. "The name suits you. You're like a little fawn."

He turned to his father and grandfather. "She's Little Fawn."

They nodded and smiled.

As night approached, Karl insisted that Little Fawn have his bed. He made himself a pallet in the corner, even though Willie offered him his bed over and over.

As he drifted off to sleep in his loft, Willie dreamed of a little fawn he had once seen near the river. He had tried to catch it and bring it home, but its need for freedom had given it strength to run away.

CHAPTER FOUR

Little Eagle

The next morning, Willie looked out of his small loft window. The snow had stopped, and the sun already struggled to burn through the clouds. Willie squinted at the bright snow, and then dressed and climbed down the ladder.

The Indian maiden was bending near the fire, stirring in a pot.

He greeted her. "Se-go-li."

She rose quickly and turned. "Se-go-li." A faint smile crossed her thin face.

Karl came in the door with an armload of wood. "She kept the fire going and found cornmeal to make a pot of mush before I got up."

Willie smiled.

"I'm trying to make her understand that we have to try and get her tribe to take her back, but I didn't have much luck."

"Will they hurt her?"

"No, but I'm not sure they'll let her stay. No harm in my trying to reason with them."

Gramps came in from tending the horses. "Not quite so cold this morning." He stomped his heavy boots on a mat. "But the vind vill cut right through you. For sure, it vill."

Willie never tired of the musical sounds his grandfather's broken English made. Every sentence was like a little song.

Karl said, "It's good the snow stopped."

Willie watched Little Fawn stirring the mush. He wished she could stay. Thoughts of his mother flooded his mind. It would be good to have a woman in the house again, even if she were just a girl-woman. He sighed heavily. It would probably not be possible.

After they had eaten, Karl and Pieter put on their heavy coats.

Willie asked quickly, "Where we going?"

Karl adjusted the coonskin cap over his bushy hair. "Over to Buster Kill to run the traps. I want you to stay here with Little Fawn."

Disappointment surged through him, but Willie swallowed hard and nodded.

Karl touched Little Fawn's shoulder. "Willie will stay with you. We'll be back soon as we can."

Her dark eyes darted from one to the other.

Gramps pulled on his leather gloves. "When ve get back, ve going to her village and talk vith her folks."

Willie sighed and looked at Little Fawn. He wondered if she understood anything they had said.

After they had left, Willie got down his knife and cedar block from the mantle and began carving.

The Indian maiden sat on a stool near the fire and watched as the chips flew.

He sighed and looked at his work. "Supposed to be a horse when I finish." He held it up. "Doesn't look much like anything now." He thought he saw her smile.

He put his knife and block aside and walked over and pulled down an old trap from the wall. "Trap. They went to check the traps. Maybe we have a beaver or two; maybe an otter or a mink." He said it as well as he could in Seneca dialect.

She nodded her understanding. He felt good that he had been able to communicate with her.

He added more wood to the fire and turned in time to see her grab at her stomach and a frown cross her face.

He sucked in his breath and went to her side. "Baby?"

She looked up at him and said not a word. He could see her swallow hard.

His heart was racing as he glanced toward the window anxiously. He found himself praying, "Oh, dear Jesus!"

Thoughts toppled over each other in his young mind. Should he go for the others or stay here with her? He knew at once he must stay with her.

He asked, "Can I help?"

She shook her head quickly and walked to Karl's bed and drew the curtain, shutting herself away from him.

He walked over and pulled the curtain back.

She flashed a threatening look and said in Indian dialect, "Go away!"

Willie dropped the curtain as if it were hot and walked back to the fire. He remembered that the women in his mother's village always had their babies alone or with other women around. His mother had told him that childbirth was a natural thing and women could do it alone if necessary. But he couldn't help feeling the sweat trickling down his skin—even though the cabin was far from warm.

He heard Little Fawn groan softly. Willie bit his bottom lip as another soft whimper eased through the drawn curtain. How he hated the helpless feeling that flooded through him. He went to the fire and pushed the iron kettle near to heat water. Maybe she would drink a cup of tea.

Soon steam rose from the spout. With a shaking hand he poured boiling water over the dried herbs.

He walked to the curtain and opened it enough to pass the cup through. "Tea?"

"Go away!"

Willie sat down and sipped at the steaming tea himself. He walked to the window again to see if Karl and Pieter were coming.

Another hour passed.

He heard a very loud groan, then a stifled scream. Then silence.

He had goose bumps all over him. "Little Fawn?"

"Go away!" This time, there was a real command in her trembling voice.

He had just started to sit down when he heard it. Chills started again, this time at the bottom of his spine. They traveled with lightning speed to the crown of his head, prickling his scalp.

The baby cried!

He laughed aloud and clapped his hands.

He yelled, "Little Fawn—Baby!"

She said the word with a gentleness that Willie had not heard since his mother died. "Baby."

He put his hand to his mouth and then laughed aloud. "A little baby!" He wanted desperately to see the child, but knew she would not let him now. There were things she must do first.

He waited for what seemed an eternity and then heard her say in dialect, "Water."

He jumped up. Did she want water to drink or warm water in a bowl? He decided to bring both.

His hands shook as he dipped a cup of water from the cedar bucket and passed it through the curtain. She took it, but repeated, "Water."

He quickly poured water from the kettle into a wooden bowl and cooled it down with cold water. He grabbed a clean towel and passed it through the curtain with the bowl of water.

She mumbled her thanks.

Willie waited and heard her talking softly to the baby. A warm feeling flooded his being. After awhile, he said out loud, "I'm going for wood."

Willie looked up the mountain trail. No sign of them yet. He walked through the deep snow to the shed where they kept the wood. He took his time, breathing in the fresh, cold air. He had begun to feel stifled inside the cabin.

Willie couldn't understand his feelings. Why did he feel like crying? Maybe it was relief; maybe the helpless feeling was finally leaving him. After wiping a tear from each cheek with his sleeve, he slowly piled his arms high with wood.

Once at the cabin, Willie kicked open the door with his foot and closed it the same way. "I'm back."

A gentle voice came from behind the curtain. "Come."

He flung the wood in the box. The excitement was almost unbearable as he slowly drew back the curtain. Little Fawn sat in a straight chair, the newborn baby wrapped in her blanket. The whole room was clean and neat.

He looked down into the face of the sleeping baby and swallowed.

He said in Seneca dialect, "Pretty baby."

She smiled and repeated, "Pretty baby."

With one finger, Willie touched the infant's soft black hair. It felt like the down on a baby bird. "Boy?"

She smiled and nodded, "Boy."

He sat on a stool and in dialect and in English, told her how he, too, had been born in that same bed. He smiled. "It must be a bed made especially for Indian babies."

She listened carefully with wide eyes. Somehow he felt she understood what he had said. "My mother called me Little Eagle because I was always climbing to the highest place around." Willie smiled, remembering one time when he had wandered off. His mother had found him atop the mountain far above the creek where they were fishing. She had scolded him gently and hugged him close, saying, "My Little Eagle."

He touched the baby's soft head once again.

Little Fawn touched Willie's hand. "Little Eagle—good."

He didn't know what to say, so he repeated, "Pretty baby."

Surely her people would want her back in the village now that she had a fine man child, who looked just like any other Indian baby.

There was certainly a lot that Willie did not know.

Willie wished he didn't feel so bad about taking Little Fawn back to her village. He turned around on his horse and watched her walk behind them on the trail, the baby fastened securely on her back. She did not want to ride, and Karl had to speak firmly from time to time to get her to ride for at least a little while behind him.

It was almost a day's ride to the Oneida village. It was nestled in a small valley on the banks of the Mohawk River.

The two weeks that Little Fawn and the baby had been with them had been good for all three Krols. It had taken their minds off the cruel war. Willie had held the baby often. He smiled, remembering how strange it felt to hold such a little person in his arms.

Little Fawn had quickly learned much of the Dutch family's language and ways. Now that she was leaving, sadness filled them all.

Willie knew it was for the best that she return to her people. She had missed them terribly. Her pretty face was sad most of the time.

Karl spoke. "I've been to this village to trade several times. Most of the tribesmen have gone to fight in the Continental army."

Pieter shifted in his saddle. "They is about the only Iroquois tribe not for the British, ain't they?"

Karl nodded. "Only because the British got to the other chiefs first, making promises they'll never keep."

Willie sighed. Maybe the Indian nations would see how wrong the Redcoats were. He looked at the high peaks about him. They were still covered with snow. The sun was bright, but the wind cut through the boy like a sharp knife. Willie pulled his bearskin coat closer around him.

Karl pointed. "The village is just ahead."

A worried look crossed Little Fawn's face. Willie felt great pity for her.

As they rode into the village, scrawny dogs barked. Women and children stepped from the doors of their longhouses and watched them curiously.

The chief and several braves stood at the end of one longhouse. Willie thought the chief had a very angry look on his face.

Karl dismounted and helped Little Fawn down. Willie tied the horses and came to his family's side. Pieter stood behind with his rifle pointed to the ground.

Karl spoke in Indian dialect. The chief motioned them into the longhouse so they could warm themselves at the small fire.

Willie's eyes darted from one to the other as they took seats inside. He saw the chief frown at Little Fawn. "You are not welcome here."

A tear rolled down both of her cheeks and she lowered her head.

Karl began, "Chief Great Bear, this woman of your tribe has a man child. I found her on the trail, nearly frozen. I took her to my home where the child was born. She misses her people."

The chief's glance was hard and unpitying as he looked at the young mother. "This was my daughter. She has shamed me. The baby's father was a white soldier."

Willie looked quickly at Little Fawn and then at his own father. She was the chief's daughter!

Karl shifted his weight and then sighed. "I didn't know she was your daughter. What's done is done. Surely you, a great chief, have forgiveness in your heart."

The baby whimpered. Little Fawn quickly took him from her back, cuddling him to her bosom.

The chief looked quickly at the baby and back to his daughter. "You can stay, but papoose must go."

Her eyes widened and more tears quickly filled them. "Papoose mine." She squeezed the baby to her. A sinking feeling came over Willie.

The chief got up and walked outside. Everyone else followed. The visit was over. He said once more, his arms folded stiffly at his chest, "Papoose must go."

Karl tried again. "The baby is part of her, and certainly a part of you. I know of other great chiefs who adopted strangers and came to love them. This baby has your blood."

Piercing eyes looked at Karl. "Different. There is shame here."

Old Pieter then tried his hand. "Can great White Spirit have forgiveness for you if you cannot forgive something which could not be helped?"

The chief looked quickly at the old man. "Great White Spirit will understand."

Willie asked the chief, "What will happen to the baby?"

"If you leave it, it will be killed, just as the soldier was killed when we found him. I want no part of him in this village."

Willie pleaded with his father. "You can't let them kill an innocent baby."

An older squaw stood nearby watching anxiously. Little Fawn kept looking at her. Finally, she walked up to her and looked into her face. The woman looked down at the child and Willie thought he saw a gentle expression cross her face. Little Fawn spoke to her and tried to hand the baby to her. The older woman backed away quickly and looked at the chief who by now was staring coldly at the pair.

Karl asked Little Fawn, "Your mother?"

She nodded sadly.

Several children came to Little Fawn and touched her long skirt. She hugged them all. How they seemed to love her!

One tried to see the baby, but the older woman rapidly said something and the child backed away quickly.

Karl walked to Little Fawn and put his arm around her thin shoulder and led her to one side.

Willie's eyes widened as he saw her hand the baby to Karl. "Take him. He will live as Little Eagle lives."

Willie swallowed hard as he heard his father say, "I can't take care of him."

"Please, find someone."

"Please, Father," Willie said, "let's take him so he can live."

Karl's face had a desperate look. He stared at the tiny baby in his big, rough arms.

Little Fawn wiped the tears that kept streaming down her face. "I just fed him. He'll be all right."

The chief was getting impatient. "Take the child and leave."

Karl said to Little Fawn, "I'll do the best I can for him." And to the chief, he said, "You are a hard man, but I understand you cannot change what is in your heart."

The chief walked back into the longhouse, and Willie went for the horses. He knew he would never, as long as he lived, forget the heartbreaking expression on Little Fawn's face as they rode out of the village with her baby.

On the trail, Willie held the sleeping baby. Running Wind did not feel the extra passenger, but seemed to know that the ride must be smooth so as not to awaken him.

Karl said, "Katrina Mueller's young baby died recently from a fever. Maybe she will help us. Their place is only a few hours from here."

Willie brightened. He liked the kindly woman who lived over the mountain. She had a son named Joshua who was about his age. Some said he was backward, but Josh was an expert shot and could skin a deer with lightning speed. Yes, Mrs. Mueller just had to help them. She just had to.

CHAPTER FIVE

Summer—1777

Willie watched his grandfather knead the stiff dough. Pieter wasn't as good at it as Willie's mother had been, but he got the job done. There was about as much flour on the old man as in the wooden bowl.

Willie's thoughts flew to Katrina Mueller. She had taken the baby with open arms and tears of joy. He was determined to go soon for a visit. The baby must be as cute as a speckled pup by now.

"Gramps, what we need around here is a woman."

Pieter looked up. There was a dusting of flour on his spectacles. "You don't like my cooking?"

"Sure, but you could be doing more important things with your time." He smiled. "Not that keeping the three of us fed is unimportant."

"I'll say. I know who vould squeal the loudest if there was no pot on to boil every day."

Willie grinned as his grandfather mumbled something in his beloved Dutch language. He took down his cedar block and began to whittle. The sharp knife fought at the block. He hadn't worked on it since Little Fawn left. Planting and cultivating the corn, squash and beans had taken most of their spare time.

Grandfather looked at Willie and, as an afterthought, said, "Yeah, I could be doin' more important things like fighting for my country. But now I'm too old for anyting but voman's vork."

Willie frowned. "That's not true. Nobody can tan hides better than you or make a trap or build a house as good as this one."

A heavy sigh escaped the old man. "Maybe. Vere is Karl?"

"He left before first light to meet his militia outfit."

Pieter nodded and covered the bread dough with a clean cloth, setting it near the fireplace to rise. "Now I remember. A rider came by yesterday and told him Burgoyne vas still heading this vay vith 9,000 troops."

Willie was well aware of Burgoyne's army. It seemed to be all they talked about. Burgoyne's army moved not a foot that the Americans didn't know about. Spies were plentiful and eager to keep everyone abreast of the news. Of course, people knew that a lot of news was exaggerated and that some was simply not true. They wondered how much truth there was in the rumor that it took thirty carts just to haul Burgoyne and his lady's belongings and special wines. Some of the other rumors made sense, though: for example, that 240 horses were needed to drag all the artillery along, and that there were 500 carts of provisions, powder and supplies for the huge army.

Willie sighed. "I even heard that 500 soldiers' wives and children were tagging along with the army."

Gramps sniffed. "Vell, that's right. The wives do laundry, cookin' and such in return for being near their menfolks. But sure don't seem like no vay to fight a war."

Willie grinned. "Can't you just picture that mess of horses, soldiers, carts, artillery and all trying to get through the tangle of felled trees that the Americans are cutting down to slow them."

The old man chuckled. "Those bright red British uniforms won't be pretty long."

Willie pictured the felled trees across trails, the smashed bridges, and the creeks that had been dammed up to make new swamps. The Colonials had carried away or burned all the food supplies. Willie wondered how the Americans would survive when their own supplies ran out: There would be nothing to forage from.

Grandfather lit his clay pipe and puffed thoughtfully. "They can't make no more than a mile a day in those voods and this heat."

Willie held up his carving. "Does this look like a bear?"

The old man wanted to make Willie feel good, so he said, "It sure does."

Willie pretended to be hurt. "Well, it's supposed to be a horse."

"Well, vy didn't you say it vas supposed to look like a horse?"

Willie broke into laughter and the old man joined in.

When the laughter died down, Gramps said, "I tink you're more creative at the voodpile." More laughter.

Willie scooped up the cedar chips and threw them in the fire. They blazed up and he inhaled the delicious fragrance. "I think you're right, Grossvater." He stretched his tall, young frame. "I'm going to that little valley and see if those wild horses are still there."

Pieter shook his head. "Told you once them horses ain't vild. They're from the Johnson place. They turned 'em loose so's the Tories don't get 'em."

"Well, they act wild." He wiped the table getting every tiny piece of cedar chip.

"Don't take long to turn vild after not having care or regular feed."

"They look sleek and fine."

"Yeah, vell you be careful. Can't tell when a band of Tory-loving Indians might have their eye on the same horses."

"Don't you worry none. You know nobody can sneak up on an Indian."

Gramps grinned. "Unless it's another Indian. Besides, you as much Dutch as Indian, so that makes you vulnerable."

"What's vulnerable mean?"

Pieter puffed at his pipe. "Vell, in this case, it means you just as apt to get in trouble as anybody else."

Willie laughed and squeezed his grandfather's shoulder. "I'll try not to be...vulnerable."

"And don't take too long. I feel uneasy with your vater out doing God only knows vat, and you traipsing off looking for vild horses that ain't vild."

"You worry like a woman, too."

Gramps threw a dish towel playfully at his grandson. "Be back before night."

"I will."

———

As usual, Willie talked to Running Wind as they passed through a deep canyon. "If I could figure out a way to corral them, we could sell 'em to the army and get a nice piece of money." He sighed. "And we could sure use money about now."

He wondered if he could do it alone. Surely he could get at least one; maybe he'd try that.

The August sun was blistering hot, so each time they crossed a stream, boy and horse drank from the cold water. Willie swished the water on his face and arms to cool them. "Feels good!"

He sat awhile on the rocks, his feet dangling in the cold water. Running Wind picked at the green grass which poked out from between the rocks. The boy lay back on the warm rock and looked around. The Adirondacks towered on all sides. He felt so small. He held his breath as a huge eagle sailed high above him. The majestic bird screamed as it disappeared over the mountain. Willie felt compelled to say aloud, "Big eagle, Little Eagle sees you and hears your cry."

For a moment he felt silly, but then he laughed. The laugh started down deep in his stomach and bubbled up and out across the mountains, echoing wonderfully.

Running Wind stopped eating to watch him. Willie held his stomach and sat up and laughed some more. Finally, he stopped, feeling weak and spent. The young half-Indian, half-Dutch boy had no way of knowing how desperately he *needed* to laugh. Now with a sober face, he sat on the rock and sighed, not able to understand what had come over him. Whatever it was, it had caused a feeling of relief inside.

He smiled and said to Running Wind, "I acted crazy, but I'm really not, fellow." He rubbed the stallion's nose and felt the warm breath on his face. "We'll go now and see if the horses are still there."

Together, boy and horse ascended a mountain and followed the shady deer trail. Willie reached down from Running Wind's back and stripped a raspberry bush of its fruit. He plopped the berries into his mouth. The tart sweet juice ran deliciously down his throat.

By and by, he took another trail: one that would take him near the top of the mountain. He found himself holding his breath as he neared the top. Willie scanned the lush, green meadow below and his heart pounded. There they were! He quickly counted them. Still a dozen. He moved down slowly, being careful not to make a noise. He picked out the snow white stallion, standing erect with perked ears. It was already well aware of the intruders.

The boy felt the rope at his side. He wished he were full-blooded Indian so he would be fearless and could rush into the herd and take his choice, but the Dutch half of him simply would not allow such action.

He dismounted and placed a reassuring hand on Running Wind's side. "Stay here, boy."

His silent, bare feet moved quickly along the edge of the meadow. A rabbit scampered nearby. Willie jerked his head to see what it was, then turned again to look at the herd. The mares were still grazing. The white stallion walked around his harem.

Suddenly, Running Wind dashed past Willie like a streak of black light. Whinnying wildly, he ran directly toward the herd, his bridle flying in the wind.

Willie's eyes opened wide. "Whoa, Running Wind, stop!" But the great black stallion kept going full speed ahead. The white stallion circled the mares. They ran toward the opening of the small meadow, while he came to meet the black foe who dared to threaten his kingdom.

Willie ran toward them, not knowing what he could do. He realized now the terrible mistake he had made. He should have tied his horse a long way back. He had forgotten that by nature Running Wind would fight the stallion for the mares.

Now, black and white met, rearing up and biting each other. Willie was close enough now to hear the snorting and snapping of teeth. Their manes bristled and their tails were highly arched. They stood on hind legs, snorting and screaming at each other. Hooves cracked together. The stallions pounded and bit at each other's manes, while Willie yelled and tried to hit them with the coiled up rope.

Now, black and white met, rearing up and biting each other. Willie was close enough now to hear the snorting and snapping of teeth.

"Git! Stop that!" All of his efforts were like so much wind blowing. Running Wind seemed a stranger, paying no attention whatsoever to the boy's commands.

Finally, Willie landed a blow on Running Wind's neck and got his attention. The black stallion backed away momentarily. At that second, the white stallion turned and raced toward his mares, whinnying as he ran. Running Wind pawed at the ground. Willie walked to him, talking softly, and then took the reins.

Willie's heart was in his throat as Running Wind snorted to clear his nostrils. "I'll have to take the full blame, boy," Willie said gently. "I should have known better."

He examined the one break in Running Wind's skin. The horse was glistening with sweat, and saliva strung from his mouth. He still fought to catch his breath, never taking his eyes off the retreating white stallion.

Willie's legs were weak with relief that nothing more had happened. He watched with disappointment as the horses charged single-file through the narrow opening in the high mountain wall, the pounding of their hooves echoing as they fled.

He mounted Running Wind. "You're a good fighter, but if I hadn't stopped you, you might have gotten the worst end of it. Oh, you think not? Well, I think so, 'cause he had more to lose than you." He chuckled at his own joke.

As they rode out of the meadow, Willie felt a drop of rain and looked overhead at the heavy clouds. "Better get going, the bottom's fixin' to fall out." He gave one last wistful look and left the meadow behind.

Heavy drops of rain began to fall. Thunder roared across the mountains and lightning flashed. Willie rode under a nearby ledge and watched the summer storm. Dismounting, he waited for it to stop. He sat on a boulder and snapped off a nearby stalk of grass to put in his mouth. "Somehow, I've just got to get those horses before somebody else does."

As the rain poured off the overhang, the boy's thoughts went to General Burgoyne's army. A rain like this would swell the creeks and rivers, making it even harder for the army to make time.

Willie sniffed at the good, fresh smell of the rain.

Finally, after an hour or more, the rain slowed down. He knew that his grandfather was just about to put the bread on to cook in the black iron spider. His mouth watered as he thought of the wonderful aroma that would fill the cabin. The thought caused him to hurry toward home. He hoped his father had returned.

CHAPTER SIX

Grandfather Remembers

Willie picked a weed from his mother's grave. Why had God taken her from them? She had been the sunshine in the crude log cabin, singing Indian songs and baking sweet breads, and making everyone feel good whether they wanted to or not.

He jumped to his feet at a sound behind him.

His father laughed softly. "You're a lot of Indian when I can't sneak up on you."

"You walk like an ox." Willie smiled at his father.

"Oh, I do, do I?" He tousled his son's long hair. "Want to talk about her?"

Willie shrugged. Things didn't seem to be going well at all. He watched as his father sat on a nearby boulder and pulled out a clay pipe. "You know, son, I'm glad in a way that she's not here to see all this horror," Karl said, stuffing the pipe with tobacco. "She's peaceful now, and waiting for us to join her someday."

Willie looked down at the grave, trying with all his young heart to believe him. "I just miss her so much." Hot tears crowded his eyes, and he looked away quickly.

Karl didn't light the pipe, but put it back with the tobacco still in it. "I miss her, too."

"Will we ever stop missing her?"

"I hope not. Her beautiful memory—and you and father—are about all I have to keep me going in this war."

Willie sniffed and picked up a small rock, rubbing its smooth surface. "How long will the war last?"

"Well, it's hard to say, but what with this Jane McCrea incident, it might not be as long as before."

Willie had heard about the needless killing of the young woman by a group of Wyandots in Burgoyne's army. She was only twenty-three and had gone to Fort Edward to wait for her lover, a lieutenant in Burgoyne's approaching army.

In spite of threats from Burgoyne, the Indians did mostly as they pleased. There had been several stories of how the murder actually had taken place, but when the Indians returned to the British camp in late July, they had two scalps, one of which had beautiful long hair; her lieutenant immediately recognized it as Jane's.

Stories of the bloody incident spread like wildfire. The patriot cause needed a shot in the arm and the Jane McCrea incident did the trick. The New Englanders felt that if such a thing could happen to Miss McCrea, herself a Tory and the fiancée of a Tory officer, then it could well happen to them and their families. And so more Colonials came from their homes and farms, from the woods and valleys, carrying their homemade weapons to defend their country against bloodthirsty rascals like Burgoyne.

"Father, do you really think Burgoyne is that bad, to let his Indians kill that young woman?"

Karl shook his head. "No, probably not. But where his blame lies is not seeing that he had lost control. He should have just sent the Indians on their way."

Willie sighed. "Seems so wrong."

He nodded. "Much is wrong in war. For example, the Congress placing General Gates in charge over General Schuyler. To me, Schuyler is a much better commander than Gates. What we need now is someone who dares to take a chance, and 'Granny' Gates simply will not do it."

Willie smiled at the nickname given the general so recently placed in command of all the Continental armies of the north. So much had happened, and so quickly: Ticonderoga was lost to the British in July, Burgoyne was storming on toward Albany, Congress had changed commanders in the field, and now, after the Jane McCrea incident, everyone was coming to the rescue. "I'll just be glad when it's all over."

"We all will, son."

Willie's mind left the war for a moment. He looked into the distance.

Karl Krol looked at his Dutch-Indian son and smiled.

"Who *am* I, Father?" Willie said softly.

"You are William Krol, my son; and you are Little Eagle, whose mother was the daughter of a great chief." Karl paused, letting that soak in.

The boy felt a strangeness inside at being reminded that he was indeed two people.

Karl added softly, "And you are a child of God."

Willie looked across the mountains. A soft breeze blew his hair back from his face. "Are we really all children of God as the missionary taught?"

Karl nodded. "Indeed we are."

"Then why are we fighting? Why can't we have peace?"

Karl looked hard at his son. "Because there are those who want to lord it over others. Man is greedy for power. Because of this, there have always been wars and there probably always will be." He looked down a moment. "Even children of God get warped in their minds at times and forget their purpose on earth. We must do the best we can. God expects no more—and no less—from us.''

Willie listened carefully and then said, ''When I lived for that year in Mother's village, they told me to forget my Dutch heritage and think of myself only as an Indian.''

Karl stood up and stretched his tall frame. ''It's understandable for them to feel like that. But can you?''

Willie quickly shook his head. ''No, I'm proud to be your son. It's just hard at times being two people.''

Karl put his arms around Willie and hugged him close. ''Son, you are not two people. You are one very strong and intelligent person, who just happens to have the blood of two very proud races coursing through his veins. I think that makes you very special.''

Willie felt better as his father hugged him. He smelled the pipe in Karl's pocket and the sweat on the rough, homespun shirt. Suddenly, he felt strengthened.

Karl released his son and said, ''Things will get better, you'll see.''

Willie smiled at his father, who was pulling his old floppy hat down over a bushy head of hair. ''I know, Vater.''

''I'm leaving at daybreak to join my company. I might be away several weeks this time. I want you to look after your grandfather.''

Willie fought to hide his disappointment.

Karl said, ''Isolated the way we are, it isn't likely you'll have intruders. If you should and can't do better, *don't fight them.* Give them what they ask. At least you'll have a better chance of staying alive.''

The boy knew that the Indians and Tories were pillaging and killing people and then burning out the homes. "Give them everything?" he asked, wide-eyed.

"If you have to, yes. Oh, and while I'm gone, pull as much fodder as you can. Tie and stack it in the barn. Gramps will help you."

"I'll take care of everything. Don't you worry a bit."

"I won't."

But Willie knew his father would feel concern for them every minute he was gone.

———

Willie turned the thin pages of the big Dutch Bible, picking out the words he recognized, while Gramps cleaned and polished his rifle. The room was lit only by two candles.

"Dis old rifle's been a real friend to me."

When Willie didn't respond, Pieter repeated, "A really good friend." He peered over his glasses at Willie. "Did I ever tell you about the time ve outsmarted the Indians when I vas fightin' vith Rogers' Rangers?"

Willie smiled. Pieter had indeed told him many times. But with each telling there came new versions of the battle, which Gramps had either made up or had simply failed to tell before. Either way, the boy never tired of hearing the old man's tales of the French and Indian war. Fighting with Rogers' Rangers must have been the most exciting adventure anyone could have had.

"Tell me about it, Gramps." Willie closed the Bible and leaned back in his chair.

Gramps gently placed the rifle on the table and patted it. He pulled at his white moustache. "Vell, let me tell you, young man, I pray God you never see such mean tings happen as there vas in the vinter of 1758. You see, the French and Indians both hated Major Rogers. And that was 'cause he could outsmart 'em at every turn and at their own game. They made a vow to get him dead or alive; preferably dead.''

Gramps leaned forward in the chair and grasped his thin knees. ''It vas March, 1758. Ve left Fort Edward vith one hundred eighty men. Major Rogers had his orders from Colonel Haviland to reconnoiter the French position at Ticonderoga. Vell, sir, vat Major Rogers didn't know vas that Colonel Haviland's orders were known by too many people. Vord had already leaked back to the French at Ticonderoga and they vas ready for us.''

The old man laughed and leaned back and rocked vigorously in the chair, thoroughly enjoying himself. ''You'd have to know the Major to 'preciate the vay he vas. He vas so daring, it vas downright scary just to be vith him. You just didn't know vat he'd try next.''

Willie smiled. ''I wish I had known him.''

''Me too, son, 'cause you'd never forget him.''

Old Pieter continued. ''The snow vas four feet deep in places and ve all vas vearing snowshoes. After 'bout a mile or so of that hard valking, the advance guard came runnin' back telling us that about a hundred Indians vas coming our vay. Vell, sir, Major immediately laid a perfect ambush. By the time ve got *them* out of the vay, at least six hundred more Frenchmen and Indians came at us.''

He sniffed and thought a minute. ''There vasn't nothin' for us to do but break and run. Ve still lost fifty men. Ve ran far enough to where ve could hold 'em off. That whole afternoon ve fought for our lives. All those muskets crashing and Indians awhooping and men dropping like flies—it was a bad sight to see.''

In his young mind, Willie could picture it all. He leaned forward, resting his elbows on his knees.

"But you see, son, those Canadians and Indians vould have given a thousand men for Major Rogers 'cause they feared him and knew of his famous ambushes. And we fought hard 'cause we all knew we'd rather have an unmarked grave in the snow than be captured."

"Then what, Gramps?" He loved the way his grandfather's voice rose and fell, almost with a rhythm.

"It vas a true blessing that night fell. Our position on the side of the mountain vas the only ting that kept 'em from killing us all. Vell, this Lieutenant Phillips had fifteen men and they vas on the side of the mountain with about three hundred Indians surrounding them. Major Rogers shot up that mountain and saw right away there vas nothing for Phillips to do but surrender after being promised mercy. If he had known the outcome, he'd have fought to the last man. The snow around them vas already red with blood."

As Gramps rocked slowly, he continued, "Soon as Phillips and his men surrendered, they were tied to trees and chopped to death." Pieter shook his head sadly. "Major Rogers and those of us left ran like vildfire to save *our* scalps. Ve started out vith one hundred eighty good men and ended up vith forty. Ve managed to make our vay back to Fort Edward with our vounded."

He patted his rifle again. "Yes, this rifle has been a friend."

Willie watched his grandfather staring into space. "You were so proud to serve with Major Rogers, weren't you?"

Pieter nodded slowly. "Any man vould be." He paused and continued with a smile. "Then there vas the time that Rogers and his rangers slaughtered all the Frenchmen's cattle outside the fort. They left a note on the horn of an ox tanking Montcalm for the meat!"

The old man chuckled softly for a while, and then fell silent. Some moments passed before he said thoughtfully, "I vas just tinking about fightin' *vith* the British in that var and now ve're fightin' against 'em.'' He sighed heavily. ''Don't make much sense.'' Gramps ran his hand over his balding head. ''Vish I vasn't too old to fight now. I feel so useless.''

Willie's heart ached for his grandfather. ''I bet you could scout as good now as you did with Major Rogers.''

He nodded. ''I could still show your father a ting or two.''

Willie smiled. It was probably true.

Gramps stood and put the rifle over the fireplace. He faced his grandson. ''Vant me to go vith you to get those horses?''

Willie's eyes widened. ''I'd like to, but Father said for us to stay put.'' He knew that talking about the earlier war had renewed the old man's vitality.

Pieter acted as though he hadn't heard his grandson. He put his hands on his thin hips. ''Ve could get 'em easy and have 'em sold long before Karl gets back. Be some real nice money. Vat you say?'' His blue eyes twinkled in the dim light.

''Gramps, we better not. We got to finish that fodder and....''

''You vant to or not?'' Pieter's mouth tightened.

Willie swallowed. He had never disobeyed his father and— as badly as he wanted to get the horses—he would not disobey him now.

''No, Gramps, I can't. But we could go for fresh meat with my bow and arrow. It's not far down the hill where I saw some mighty big tracks....''

''Never mind. Forget it. I'm goin' to bed.''

Willie sighed. He really felt sorry for his grandfather. In his loft bed, Willie tried and tried to figure out a way to go with his grandfather to get the horses without directly disobeying Karl. He decided that he would sleep on it and see how he felt the next morning.

"Good night, Gramps. I love you."

He listened, but heard only the slow, even breathing of old Pieter Krol.

———————

Willie woke with a start and sat up in his straw bed.

"Gramps!" A strange feeling ran over him as he pulled on his pants and climbed quickly down the ladder.

He pulled the heavy curtain back from the place where Gramps slept. His bed was empty.

Steam spewed from the big iron kettle. "Guess he went outside for wood." Willie took a glance at the full wood box and rushed outside still rubbing the sleep from his eyes. "Gramps, where are you?" he shouted.

Running to the edge of the woods, Willie looked down the path toward the spring, then back to the trail.

He scanned the trampled grass, then realized that his grandfather had gone down the trail on horseback.

The boy's heart raced as he ran back in the cabin. He pushed the fire back further in the fireplace. Then he took down his musket and powder horn. Surely Gramps hadn't gone for the wild horses alone. No, he didn't really know where they were.

Where could he be? He buckled his belt and pushed the knife into the scabbard, thinking all the while of a million awful things that could have happened.

Running Wind was in the stable alone, moving about nervously. Willie spread a colorful blanket across the horse's back and quickly mounted. The trail was almost cold; his grandfather had surely left at first light.

Willie fought at his near panic. Grandfather could probably take care of himself, but his senses weren't as keen now. He didn't hear well; that one handicap could easily mean disaster.

The boy scanned the high mountains on all sides for danger. The trail grew fainter though the sun climbed higher. A rock lay in the trail where a horse's hoof had moved it in passing. The boy's sharp eyes missed nothing.

He came to a small waterfall and dismounted, letting his horse drink. He concentrated on other sounds than the water rushing downward. The wind rustled the leaves on the oaks and swished at the tall pines. A squirrel chattered, and a blue jay scolded an army of crows cawing in a nearby grove of white birch.

He sniffed at the air. Smoke! Maybe a campfire. Whose? His grandfather's? Indians? Tories?

Willie's heart quickened as he jumped astride his horse and continued over the almost disappearing trail. He saw a spot where a fallen leaf had been crushed into the scant soil by a horse's hoof less than an hour ago. It would have gone unnoticed by anyone else.

Running Wind perked his ears, then whinnied.

"Shhh!" Willie cocked his head to one side. The stallion continued to whinny. The boy clutched his primed musket. He looked quickly at the craggy, wooded range of mountains to his left and to the high green crest of another range to his right, but saw nothing.

A soft wind was at his back, and he sniffed again and quietly picked his way through the rocky terrain. He felt the tingling of readiness for fight or flight. He breathed through his nose with great effort to be even quieter. The hand gripping the musket was wet with sweat.

He sucked in his breath at the sight before him: Not fifty yards away his grandfather's mare grazed beside a creek.

He chanced a call. "Gramps, where are you?"

He listened. Nellie lifted her head and looked at him. Willie slid from his stallion and walked up to the still-saddled mare, looking in every direction.

"Gramps!"

His heart leaped into his throat, almost choking him. The old man lay in a crumpled heap near a giant oak. "Gramps!"

The boy ran to his side and gently turned him over. He knew at once that Pieter Krol was dead. An arrow was in his chest.

Hot tears scalded Willie's eyes and ran down his face. "Gramps, Gramps! Oh, Gramps!"

He felt again and again for signs of life, but knew there were none. The arrow had done its job well.

Willie sank under the tree and held the body in his arms. Heavy sobs competed with the sounds of the woods and the nearby waterfall.

Through tears, he examined the arrow once more. He could not recognize which tribe it had come from. He lay the old Dutchman gently on the ground and with both hands broke the arrow that he could not bear to pull out. He threw the broken arrow on the ground. The ache in his heart kept producing more tears. He did not stop them from pouring down his face.

Willie took off his shirt and placed it over his grandfather's face. He examined the smoldering campfire and guessed that the old man had stopped to rest. Willie could not stop the groaning sound that came from his lips. He walked about not knowing what to do next.

He saw the remains of a rabbit his grandfather had cooked over the small fire. The fire...it must have been that which had attracted the murderers.

But why hadn't they taken his horse? Horses were about the most important commodity around. He looked quickly at Nellie. The saddlebag was gone and so was the cherished rifle.

The killers must have surprised the old man; nothing indicated a struggle. Willie came to the conclusion they had just killed Pieter, quickly grabbed the gun and bag and left. Probably they were traveling light, or maybe they had heard him coming. They had not bothered to scalp the almost bald victim, and for that Willie was grateful.

He did not know how long he stayed at the spot, watching, figuring and aching. The task of taking his grandfather home and burying him still lay before the young boy. If only his father were here! Willie took a deep breath. He would just have to do the best he could. He picked up the broken arrow and put it in his shoulder bag. With an aching heart, he laid his grandfather's body across the saddle. Tears blinded his every step home.

Willie sat for a long time beside the fresh grave. His arms and back ached from the task of digging the unyielding, rocky soil. He thought of everything he could about his grandfather, as though eulogizing his long life. If only he could make time go backwards and do more for the old man. But he could not.

His tears had run dry, but in their place, a dull ache lay heavy in his chest, and a desperate urge to avenge his grandfather's murder.

He lifted himself slowly from the ground and looked at the full moon which lit the tiny valley. The whippoorwills kept up their constant plaintive cry, unaware of the tragedy.

From nowhere a cloud eased over the moon and a soft wind blew through the boy's hair, which was as dark as the night. He walked slowly from the birch grove carrying the shovel and musket.

On the porch, he stood a long while gazing up the hill at the two graves. His head ached with thoughts of what he must do tomorrow.

CHAPTER SEVEN

The Search Begins

Willie sat at the big oak table and stared at the quill, ink and paper before him. He heaved a sigh and picked up the quill. Dipping it slowly into the ink, he began to write.

Dear Father,
    Gramps was killed. I buried him beside Mother.
    I could not stay here. I am coming to look for you.
I will explain when I see you.

Your son,
Willie

He looked at the note so laboriously written and read it over. Not much to say for all that had happened. He wanted to put the date on the note, but he did not know what day it was.

He hid the few family possessions in a hole under the floor, carefully covering the trapdoor with a rug his mother had made. He pulled the heavy table back over it and set the crude chairs in place.

Willie tried not to look at his grandfather's rocking chair, but his eyes kept going to it as though drawn by some invisible force.

Finally, when he figured that everything had been done, the boy stood a moment in the open door. He slung his knapsack over his shoulder. He hoped he was doing the right thing. He remembered his father's words: Always make the decision that feels right at the time; then stick by it no matter how many doubts creep in. But nothing felt right just now. He only knew that he could not stay here. He had to find his father!

At the stable, he said to Nellie: "Well, girl, I'm going to set you free to forage for yourself. You'll be all right." He stroked her mane. "Maybe you'll find those other horses, or someone will find you and be good to you." The mare nodded her head up and down. Willie smiled. "You act just like you understand."

This time, she nodded up and down more vigorously. Willie laughed aloud. In spite of his grief and fear, the laughter felt good. He hugged the mare to him, and then patted her rump. "Go make yourself a new life."

Running Wind watched with interest. "No, you can't go with her. You have to go with me."

He mounted his horse and watched as Nellie stopped and looked back at him and then at the distant mountains.

"Go ahead, Nellie. You're free!"

She ran toward the lower meadow and disappeared behind a knoll.

"Maybe she'll stay close. If not, it'll all work out. Everything usually does." As he rode out of the yard, he thought of what he had just said—about everything working out. Maybe it really would. He just had to believe it.

The day was still young as he rode slowly over the Indian trail toward the Mueller's house. Maybe they had seen his father. His plan was to continue on from the Mueller's to the army fort. Perhaps his father was still there: At least they might know where he was.

A great surge of loneliness swept over him. He tried to sweep the desperately dark feeling from his mind. If only I had gone with him after the horses, Willie thought, Gramps would still be alive. He shook his head to dislodge the sickening thought. He had made a decision and stuck by it just as his father had taught him to do. But the pain that had come from that decision was almost more than the boy could bear.

The broken arrow was in his shoulder bag. He didn't know why he had brought it along. Maybe to show his father.

He sniffed and began singing a little song his father had taught him about the war. His mother had always told him to sing in times of sadness or fear. The song was called "The World Turned Upside Down."

IF the buttercups buzzed after the bee;
IF boats were on land and churches at sea;
IF ponies rode men, and
IF grass ate the cow,
IF cats should be chased into holes by the mouse;
IF mamas sold their babies to gypsies for half a crown;
IF summer was spring and the other way 'round,
THEN all the world would be turned upside down.

It was a silly song but it seemed to fit his mood. He hummed the tune for awhile. "The world is sure turned upside down, Running Wind. But I guess you don't know anything about that, do you?" He rubbed the stallion's neck.

Willie rode all morning, choosing less traveled trails and purposely avoiding the spot where he'd found his grandfather.

The late August sun blazed down on his back. He pulled off his deerskin shirt and draped it across the horse. He shifted the knapsack often and, almost as often, moved the musket from one hand to the other.

At every cool brook he stopped, and he and the horse drank deeply. At one point, he pulled back his hair and tied it with a length of rawhide.

It was getting on toward evening. Willie stopped atop a little knoll and scanned the mountains for danger. He could see the Mueller house at the bottom of the hill.

As he neared the cabin, a dog barked and Running Wind perked his ears. "It's all right," Willie said reassuringly. "Just old Shag telling 'em somebody's comin'."

He called as he rode toward the clean swept yard. "Mrs. Mueller, Josh!"

Seconds later, the door creaked open. A small, pretty woman with heavy blonde hair around her shoulders stood in the doorway holding a musket. "Who's that?" she said suspiciously. Then seeing him, she smiled, "Oh, it's Willie Krol."

"Yes, Ma'am. It's me."

The dog kept barking.

"Hush, Shag. Willie, you just put your horse in the stable and come on in."

Josh came from behind her, smiling timidly. He was a head taller than his mother. "Hello, Willie."

"Howdy, Josh."

Later, inside the rough cabin, Katrina picked up the Indian baby from his pallet on the floor.

Willie smiled. "He's really grown a lot. What did you name him?"

"Adam."

"Nice name. Did you give him an Indian name, too?"

"No, would you like to give him one?"

Willie took the baby and shook him gently on his knee. The baby laughed and cooed. "No, I think Adam Mueller is plenty of name."

She took the baby from Willie. "Adam and Josh are the brightness of my life."

Josh smiled and tucked his head, embarrassed.

Willie could wait no longer. He heaved a sigh and told them about his grandfather.

Katrina listened with sad eyes and Josh kept his head down, folding and unfolding his long arms.

She said, "Willie, I'm so very sorry. You've been through too much. My heart aches for you."

Willie swallowed. "I'll find out who killed him, and I'll kill them."

The woman shook her head quickly. "No, that's not the way, Willie. You can't take revenge. It would make you the same as them. Let God take care of it."

She reached over and touched his hand. "You'll see."

"But why'd they kill an old man? He didn't bother them."

He felt Josh looking at him.

Katrina said sadly, "Who knows why one man kills another? It's a cruel and desperate war."

Josh said in a slow, measured voice. "Pa might be dead, too."

Willie looked quickly at Mrs. Mueller for an explanation.

She nursed the baby, rocking back and forth in a straight chair. "We don't know that, Josh. I've put it all in God's hands."

Willie asked, "What does he mean?"

She sighed and stroked the baby's head. "He was supposed to come back before now, but we've had no word from him. He was scouting up near Ticonderoga."

Willie leaned forward in his chair. "Isn't my father in his company?"

She shook her head. "To tell you the truth, I don't know. I think they split up. Some were going to the rear of Burgoyne's army. Your pa might be with the others who are going ahead felling trees and making it as hard as they can for the British to get through."

She placed the sleeping baby on the bed and covered him with a blanket. "We can't suppose anything. Just have to hope and pray."

Josh said bravely, "They better not kill my pa."

Firmly Katrina said, "Enough of that, now. Let's eat some." She stirred the contents of a small black pot which hung over the fire.

"I ain't hungry," Willie tried to say. "I had berries just now."

She looked at him quickly. "Berries, my word. There's plenty, and you need to eat more than berries."

Willie didn't want to eat up their vittles, but Katrina persisted. He gave in and ate a small bowl of the fish chowder and beans. It tasted so good, he could have eaten much more but forced himself to be satisfied.

Later, Katrina said, "Willie, you stay the night here and you can go to the fort first thing in the morning to look for Karl."

"I don't want to be a bother."

She pulled her long hair back. "Land sakes, Willie, it's no bother. You can sleep over near Josh's bed. Now, it's settled."

"Can I help get the wood and water?"

Josh said quickly, "I already did it."

Willie smiled at his friend. "All right, but I want to get an early start in the morning."

Suddenly, the dog barked. The three exchanged glances.

Willie jumped up, took his musket from the corner and checked the knife in his scabbard.

Katrina blew out the candle.

Willie jumped up, took his musket from the corner and checked the knife in his scabbard. Katrina blew out the candle. Willie opened the door a crack and listened. He closed it quickly. "Sounds like two horses."

Willie opened the door a crack and listened. He closed it quickly. "Sounds like two horses."

The dog barked as though he would tear up the ground. Willie's heart picked up speed. The cabin was quiet except for the popping fire, which lit the room dimly.

A voice outside said, "Shut up, dog. Hello in there."

They said nothing. A loud knock sounded on the door.

Katrina whispered, "Ask who it is."

Willie swallowed to wet his mouth. "Who is it?"

"Long live the king."

Willie looked at Katrina, who had walked over to stand near the sleeping baby. "See what they want."

He opened the door. Two men in woodsmen's garb stood there. One had a bushy, dirty beard and the other had a grizzly growth on his face.

Out of the corner of his eye, Willie saw Katrina lighting the one candle again. "What do you want?"

The bearded one spoke. "We said, long live the king." He stared coldly at the three, who said nothing.

The two pushed their way past Willie. "I guess you ain't for the king living long, huh?"

Still, no one spoke.

One of the strangers was wearing a coonskin cap. He laughed and said in a gravelly voice, "What have we here? An Injun, a yellow-haired woman and a little baby. Looks like an Injun baby."

Willie's eyes darted around the room. Where was Josh? The cabin's back door stood slightly ajar.

The baby awoke and started to cry at all the commotion. Katrina picked him up. "What do you want? We have nothing of value."

One said with sarcasm, "I wouldn't say that. It's all accordin' to what you call valuable." He touched her hair. Katrina jerked away and stepped back.

Willie felt nauseated. One of the Tories was so close he could smell the man's sour breath.

"Halfbreed, what you doing here with this purty white woman?"

With deliberation Willie said, "We have nothing. Go, and leave us in peace."

The Tory laughed. Willie felt his finger rubbing against the trigger of his musket.

"Shut up, Injun. Speak when spoken to." With one quick movement, he snatched the musket from Willie's hand and slapped him hard across the face. Willie tightened his jaw at the pain.

Katrina said, "There's only a small amount of corn and some beans. Take it and go."

Willie repeated, "Then leave us in peace."

"I told you to shut up, Injun." The man raised his hand. Willie threw up his arm to ward off the blow.

The Tory faked a vulgar laugh. "How'd you like it, Injun, if I was to scalp you just like you do white folks?" He took Willie by his hair and jerked hard, pulling a tomahawk from his belt. The other Tory—the one holding the pistol—laughed.

Katrina yelled, "Stop, murderers! Leave the boy alone."

The baby cried louder and the dog barked feverishly, scratching at the door to get inside.

Every muscle in Willie's body tensed as he waited for the split second when the Tory would be unaware.

The man turned Willie's hair loose and backed a couple of steps away. Taking the pistol from the other man, he pointed it in the boy's face. "I think I'm gonna shoot me an Injun."

Willie's eyes darted and he lunged forward, knocking the man off balance. The Tory staggered while his companion tried to get around behind Katrina, shoving her to one side.

Suddenly, a blast filled the room. The man beside Willie crumpled to the floor, choking from the wound in his neck.

The other turned quickly to see who had fired the deadly shot.

Josh stood in the open back doorway holding a smoking musket.

The Tory pointed the pistol toward Josh, but he was not fast enough. Willie, knife drawn, knocked him to the floor.

Katrina screamed, "No, Willie!"

Josh shouted, "Kill him, Willie! Kill him!"

Katrina screamed again. "Hush, Josh! Let him go and take the other one with him."

Willie moved away from him as the man staggered to his feet and started toward the door. "Take your friend with you."

He glared at Willie as he looked down. He grabbed the dead man under the shoulders and dragged him out the door.

Josh moved to one side and stared at the man he had killed. A strange look crossed his face, as though the truth had just hit him.

The dog continued to bark as the Tory hoisted the dead man over his horse and started up the trail, still mumbling to himself.

Willie closed the heavy door and sighed as Katrina walked to her son. Without a word, she looked up into his face and squeezed his arm. None of them would sleep very soundly.

CHAPTER EIGHT

Reunions

As Willie neared the army fort, Katrina Mueller's words came back to him: "Let the sentry know right away that you're half white. There's so much hatred for the Indians since the Jane McCrea murder."

Willie knew that Katrina meant well, but deep inside his young heart a certain amount of resentment stirred. If everyone could just accept the fact that there were good and bad Indians, just as with white people. He sighed heavily, trying very hard to remember his father's words about how lucky he was to be both Dutch and Indian. Right now, he didn't feel so lucky.

He came upon a heavily rutted wagon road and was keenly aware of danger. The sun was behind him now, and his shirt clung to his wet back. He felt Running Wind's sweaty hide through the blanket.

Two soldiers on horseback rounded the curve in the road ahead. They stopped when they saw Willie and quickly drew their pistols, aiming from the waist.

"Hello there," he called.

They rode toward him with pistols still aimed. "What you want here, Injun?" one asked gruffly.

Willie licked his dry lips. "I'm William Krol, and I'm looking for my father. He's...."

He was interrupted by a sarcastic, "Ain't nobody in this Continental army who'd be *your* father, Injun."

Willie swallowed. "My father is a white man by the name of Karl Krol."

With hardly a change of expression, both men shook their heads. One said, "Don't know him. You'd best be on your way."

The other softened. "Your ma was an Injun?"

They put their pistols away, and Willie nodded. "Seneca." He almost told them she was a chief's daughter but decided not to share that precious fact with these two. Still, he continued hopefully. "My father is a patriot in the militia. Came here about a week ago. He's tall, has dark bushy hair and wears a black patch...."

One interrupted as he scratched his head. "Think I saw him in camp a few days back."

Excitement filled Willie's stomach. "Is he still here?"

"No, but there's a fella here who was with him; might know where he went. Come with us."

"Thank you."

The two looked at each other, surprised at the boy's manners.

Willie felt sheer relief flood his being at the thought that he might find his father, but the news he had for Karl burned into the boy's heart like fire.

Fort Miller served as a temporary stopover. A small detachment was encamped here, and Willie could see that they were getting ready to move out. Several permanent structures inside a tall log stockade were about all that would remain once the detachment moved on. Two cannons pointed upriver through the high walls.

One of the soldiers pointed. "That tall, lanky fella over there. He was the one with your pa."

"Thank you very much."

Willie quickly dismounted and walked up to the man, "Good afternoon, sir."

The man jerked around. Willie sucked in his breath. It was Horace Cuyler, the man who had befriended him in Albany. He couldn't find his voice, he was so surprised.

Horace broke into laughter when he saw Willie. "Well, Willie, my friend. What on earth brings you so far from home?" The green woolen cap sat at an angle on his head as he shook hands with the boy.

Willie finally found his voice. "Am I proud to see you, Horace!"

"Well, same here. Sit a spell." Horace turned to his fire and tested a chunk of meat he was cooking over a spit. "Just about ready. You're hungry, I know."

"I sure am, if you have any to spare."

"You know what the Good Book says about casting your bread on the water: It'll come back to you a hundredfold." Horace chuckled.

Willie nodded though he wasn't quite sure what it meant. He figured it meant sharing, though.

Horace pulled his knife from the scabbard and sliced a big piece of the golden brown meat, handing it to Willie. "Seen your pa a couple of days back."

Willie chewed slowly to make the food last longer. "I need to find him real bad." Before he could stop himself, he told Horace all about his grandfather, the killing at the Muellers and his desperation at having had to face it all alone.

The older man listened, chewing slowly. "Your pa's gone on toward Saratoga to get ready for the big battle. I just got back from scouting upriver. Burgoyne's moving slowly. Must be at least twenty or thirty miles back."

Willie nodded. "How far ahead you think Pa is by now?"

Horace sliced another piece of meat for each of them and pushed his coffee pot closer to the small fire. He took a bite of meat before answering. "No more than a day's ride. They're still felling trees across the trails to slow old Burgoyne. We'll all join up with General Gates at Saratoga to get ready to greet Gentleman Johnny."

"Should have left General Schuyler in charge," Willie said.

Horace shook his head. "Yep, but old Granny Gates played politics and had Schuyler ousted. They're fools if they think Gates will do a good job. All he figures to do is avoid a battle."

"Father thought General Schuyler was doing a good job."

"He was, a mighty good job. Schuyler knows strategy: how to pull it all together and make things happen. Gates is no man for the battlefield, but they'll learn that lesson too late, I reckon."

It was hard for the boy to understand grown-ups sometimes. His father always said when something is working well, don't change it. So why did they pull General Schuyler when he was doing a good job?

Horace said, "I'm going to ride point for this outfit when it moves out. Want to come along with me? We'll eventually find your father."

Relief flooded the boy. "I sure do."

Horace stretched his long, lanky body.

Willie stood up. "I won't be no trouble to you."

"Didn't figure you would. I ain't got time for no babies on this trip." Willie searched for a smile but found none.

"Yes, sir," he said straightening his shoulders. At that moment he felt like the furthest thing from a baby.

The companions stayed on the road when possible, but more often than not it was easier to ride the animal trails high above the banks of the Hudson River.

"You're mighty quiet, Willie."

He sniffed. "Guess I have a lot on my mind that needs sorting out."

"After all you've been through, I can believe that."

Willie stroked his horse's neck. "I didn't know I could do the things I did."

"Try not to think so steady on it, boy."

Willie wished he could forget it for just a short while, but it seemed to cling like a vine around his heart.

"Your father's a good man, Willie."

He nodded. "And he's strong, too."

Horace threw back his head and laughed. "I'll say he is. I saw him single-handedly lift a wagon on one end so he could work on a wheel. Wasn't nobody near to help him, but he had it up resting on a stump before I could get to him."

Willie smiled. "And he really cares a lot about our country, too."

"We all do, son. That's why we're beatin' our brains out trying to stop the British."

They rode down a grassy slope to the river to let the horses drink. "We can rest here a spell." With that remark, Horace dismounted, stripped off his shirt and splashed the cold water on his lean upper half.

Willie did the same. He watched as Horace snatched off his green woolen cap, revealing a bald head.

Willie fought back a smile. "You ain't got a smidgin of hair on your head."

"Gits in my way so I keep it shaved." He splashed water on his shining head and rubbed it dry with his bare hands.

Willie snickered. "No Indian would pride himself with your scalp."

Horace grinned, "Another good reason for keeping it shaved."

They laughed together.

Horace plunged the wool cap in the rushing water and then plunked it, still wet, on his head.

Through laughter, Willie said, "I'll cut my hair like that some day maybe."

Wide-eyed, Horace replied playfully, "Then the gals won't like you."

"They like you, Horace?"

A big smile filled his homely face. "Some do. You got a girl?"

"Don't know no girls." Willie picked up a rock and threw it into the river.

"Well, with that handsome face, you will some day."

Willie shrugged. "Maybe." He skipped a rock across the river.

Horace tilted his head to listen.

"What is it?" Willie asked quickly.

"Just listening to see if I can hear our soldiers coming."

"I don't hear them."

"Guess they're too far back. We might better slow up some."

They mounted and rode along slowly for awhile. "You like to fight, Horace?"

"You mean like in battle?" The man nodded. "Yeah, I guess I do. Leastwise, I like the challenge since it's on me to fight. But,

I'd rather have peace and save my fighting energy for hunting food and clearing land.''

Willie sighed. ''You know my problem? I feel sorry for everybody—Indians, the British and the Americans. I feel sorry for the Indian because he's so misunderstood and has had so many of his rights taken away; then, I feel sorry for the British 'cause a lot of them are too young to die, and they're so far from their homes and families; and surely for the Americans who only want to be free to make this new country of theirs grow.''

Horace listened, but made no comment. He wanted the boy to continue.

''Then, I get all mixed up with hate inside me. Hate for that person who killed my poor old grandfather who did nobody any harm; and hate for the Tory who tried to kill me just because I'm part Indian.'' He shook his head and looked down.

Horace knew it was time for him to comment. ''I guess I can understand your feelings. It's called sorting things out, gettin' the important things in their right place in your head.''

''Guess I wouldn't make a very good soldier, feeling sorry for everybody, huh?''

Horace bit his bottom lip and then said, ''On the contrary, I 'spect you'd make a fine soldier. What you have is called *compassion*. Without it or at least a little of it, a man'd be no more than a rock. Me, well, I feel sorry for wild animals tryin' to make it through the winter without starvin'. But, mind you, if a bear came at me, I'd have to fight to the bitter end, no matter how sorry I felt for him or his kind. And if somebody drove a herd of horses through the cornfield you'd worked and sweated for to have your winter eatin', you'd have to try and stop them, no matter what. Right?''

Willie understood. He nodded slowly.

"Well, sir, it's about the same with war. You have to remember we're fighting not just for cornfields, but for a way of life. We can't grow and expand in our new country with the British taxing us down to our shoe soles and destroyin' all we're trying to build on. So, compassion is good, but just don't let it get in the way of reasoning things out proper like."

The boy was truly amazed at the way this man had of making him come to terms with himself.

"You think a lot like my father," he said.

Horace chuckled. "Guess we come from the same school."

———————————

They rode silently for a while past burned-out homesteads and fields left by refugees fleeing to Albany. They were a grim reminder of the cruel war. Willie turned his face toward the river to avoid the devastation.

Suddenly, he said, "I hear voices."

Horace nodded. "I also hear axes ringing. Think we found those devils, boy. The ones we lookin' for." He chuckled.

"You mean my father's unit?"

"The very same ones."

They rode into the open toward the sweating bare backs of the workmen. Willie scanned the faces that looked their way. Suddenly, a huge tree cracked and groaned. Somebody yelled, "Timber!" Willie and Horace moved quickly to dodge the great tree. It fell, all but covering the road for many yards.

Chills of happiness raced over Willie as he picked out the huge figure of his father walking among the timber, an ax over his shoulder.

"Father!"

Karl looked up and squinted in the afternoon sun. He rushed to greet them, jumping over logs and tangles of brush. "Willie! What on earth you doing here?"

The boy jumped from his horse and ran to meet his father. As they embraced, Karl looked into his son's face. "What in heaven's name you doin' here, boy?" Then he looked up to see Horace.

"I brought him, Karl," Horace said simply.

Karl needed more answers. "Willie, I thought I told you to stay..."

"Gramps is dead, Father." Tears gained control and spilled down the boy's brown face.

Karl swallowed hard and let go of his son's shoulders. He sat down heavily on a log. With his head in his hands, he listened as Willie tearfully told the story of his grandfather's murder. The boy pulled the broken arrow from his pack and handed it to his father.

Karl took it in his big, calloused hands, turning it over and over. Willie sat next to his father and stared at the ground. There was nothing left to say.

Finally, the boy turned to Karl. "I didn't know what else to do. I left a note for you in case I missed you."

Karl put his hand on Willie's knee and squeezed. "You did the right thing, son. It's all right. I'm just sorry you had to go through it by yourself."

"I did all I knew to do."

"You did as good as any grown man could do, son."

"Who would kill Gramps, Father?"

Willie saw tears in his father's eyes as Karl said, "Who knows. Probably renegade Indians after that gun."

Willie glanced up to see Horace standing to one side. He knew they needed to be alone.

Karl looked off into the distance. "Poor old man. To have to die like that. Probably wanted to do his bit. Guess he thought it better to risk the trail than to die kneading bread dough like a woman." His voice cracked. Willie felt a tug at his own heart.

"Maybe if I'd gone with him to try and catch those horses, he'd still be alive. He all but begged me to go with him, but I wouldn't disobey you, Father."

Karl looked solemnly into his son's face. "Don't try to figure it out, son. You did what you thought was right. No use in trying to find ways to blame yourself. You ain't at fault."

When Willie did not respond, his father said firmly, "You hear me?"

"Yes, sir." Still, he wished the thought would stop eating at him.

They sat awhile talking about Gramps' life in America.

Finally, when Horace figured they'd had enough time alone, he sauntered up to them. "You going home with him, Karl?"

Karl looked up at his friend. "We got a job to do here."

Willie asked suddenly, "How'll the soldiers and the refugees traveling with them get over the road with all the trees felled across?"

Horace answered, "They'll cross at a narrow spot upriver and cut the trees behind them. Then they'll head over the mountains and circle back into the Hudson Valley."

Karl said pensively, "I'd sure like a runner to tell me just how far Burgoyne is by now, and how many troops he has left. I hear that they're dropping like flies in this heat."

"What about the rear scouts?" Horace suggested.

Karl shook his head. "God only knows when they'll get around Burgoyne's troops, if at all."

Willie said quickly, "Let *me* go back and check on Burgoyne's army."

Karl looked quickly at his son. "No. You're all I have. I can't risk you gettin' killed, too."

Horace said, "Ain't none of my business, Karl, but this Indian son of yours is not likely to get killed just scoutin'. Besides, don't you think he deserves a chance to act like a man after what he's been through?"

Karl let the words soak in. With a heavy sigh, he agreed. "Maybe you're right, Horace." He squeezed Willie's shoulder. "By now, I shouldn't doubt your ability to do almost anything, son."

Willie's heart raced with excitement as he listened to his father's words. "All I want you to do is get close enough to see about how many troops we have to deal with and what shape they're in. Then you hightail it back in this direction. If you run into our scouts, stick with them. You hear?" Willie felt his father's fingers dig into his shoulders. "You hear me, boy?"

"Yes, sir, I will."

Horace put some food into Willie's shoulder bag and said, "Be all Indian this trip, Willie, and don't override your horse."

Nodding, the boy mounted his horse. Karl repeated, "All Indian this time." He managed a small smile as he patted his son's leg.

Willie began to move out of the clearing. He looked back only to wave good-bye, turning just in time to see Karl throwing the broken arrow as far as he could.

CHAPTER NINE

Captured!

Willie glanced at the sun as it threatened to sink behind a mountain. He had to hurry and get through the tangle of forest before nightfall. All senses alert, he knew that the advance scouts of Burgoyne's great army could be anywhere. He certainly did not want to meet up with them.

An owl gave a lonely hoot, and another across the river answered. A colony of crows quarreled in a nearby grove as they readied themselves for the night. The warm wind swished Willie's long hair and cooled the sweat on his neck.

The sun, on its way to light another world, eased gently behind the mountain. Willie rode down a steep embankment to the river. It was narrow enough to cross, but he was concerned about the undercurrents that could drown both him and his horse. He swallowed hard and mentally prepared himself to cross. "You're in charge now, Running Wind." He gave the horse free rein, holding the bridle lightly.

He held his musket high, and the horse began to swim. He buckled his legs tightly around Running Wind as the water eased to his waist. Only the stallion's mighty head was above the muddy, swirling river.

"Come on, boy, you can do it."

Willie tried to keep his eye on the other shore, but found it far from easy; he was straining to hold the musket out of the water.

Without warning, the horse swerved and Willie started to slide off. The current! He felt it tugging at his legs as Running Wind fought to get his footing. Willie clung to the horse's neck. The current fought to snatch his now-drenched musket from him.

With a sudden move, the horse fought his way free of the current and regained his balance. Together horse and rider came out onto the opposite shore.

Running Wind shook himself, while Willie staggered to his feet, coughing out the water he had taken in. After catching his breath, he looked at the horse who now was nosing his shoulder. "We made it, boy. We made it."

Willie examined his water-soaked musket and the powder horn around his shoulder. He sighed heavily. "Not much good for a while now. All soaked."

He stood and looked around. It would be better traveling on this side. A full moon had risen over the mountain. Willie breathed a sigh. There would be enough light for him to go farther upriver before stopping for the night.

Dawn was just breaking as Willie peeked through the bushes at the sight below him. Soldiers, tents, horses, cattle, pieces of artillery and wagons were spread out for several miles along the river; bateaux* lined the shores. Willie reckoned this to be the main army. The boy's heart pounded in his chest as he scanned the camp, moving about slowly and carefully to get a better look.

---

*bateaux—flat-bottomed boats

In time of war and crisis, experience is almost a virtue. Willie possessed very little, for he had not lived many years. He did not see that even higher up than he, a sentry stood on a huge rock that overlooked the camp.

Willie tethered his horse and prepared to move downhill to get a better look. He almost jumped out of his skin as a booming voice above him exploded: "Halt or I'll shoot!"

Willie looked up slowly toward the voice. An Indian in a British uniform stood tall on the high rock, with a Brown Bess musket pointed right at him. Another Redcoat appeared behind Willie as though coming from nowhere. The boy rose slowly and swallowed.

The soldier near him said with a heavy British accent: "You planning to capture the King's army all by yourself, lad?"

Willie said nothing but stared coldly as shivers of fear crept from his feet to his scalp. The soldier commanded. "Speak up. You do speak the King's English, don't you?"

Still, he said nothing. The soldier yelled to the Indian. "Stay put. I'm taking this one to camp. Be on guard, there might be others." Only Willie's eyes moved, looking frantically for a split second chance to make a run for it.

"Get your horse and lead him, and don't try anything or I'll blow you to smithereens."

He glanced at his musket, leaning against a rock, still wet and useless. The soldier said quickly, "Get the musket and keep the barrel pointed to the ground. Come along, hurry up. Bring it to me."

Willie did exactly as he was told. The soldier snatched the musket and looked it over. "Looks like you swam the river with this one. You carry it. It's useless."

As they came into camp, the young boy thought it surely covered as much space as a city. He felt lightheaded from the excitement and from the sights before him. Early risers taunted him, but he paid no heed.

The soldier stopped outside a tent as large as Willie's house. "Tie your horse there and come with me."

He held the flap open for Willie to go in ahead of him. Fear filled his heart as he wondered what they would do with him.

A white-wigged officer sat with a very pretty lady at a linen covered table. They were having breakfast.

"I'm very sorry for the early intrusion, General Burgoyne," the soldier said politely.

The general looked from one to the other. "I do not wish to be disturbed while dining, Sergeant." He took a bite of food from a china plate and then sipped from a tiny cup.

"We could come back later, sir."

He waved his hand. "The damage is already done. What is it? Who is this Indian boy?"

"Found him peering down into camp. He looks to have white blood. Can't get him to speak."

Willie saw the woman looking at him and tucked his head.

"Very well," the general sighed. "Leave us be."

The soldier snapped to attention and left the tent.

Willie wondered if they could hear his heart beating, it was thumping so loudly. So this was the famous Gentleman Johnny.

The general sighed again. "So you do not speak English. French? German? How about your own Indian dialect?"

Willie looked up and into the handsome face of the general. He watched the man straighten a lacy cuff and then sip from the tiny cup once more. The general's brow furrowed as he waited for a reply.

"Surely we can find some language you speak." Burgoyne's full mouth curled at the corners. "No?"

Willie tethered his horse and prepared to move downhill to get a better look. He almost jumped out of his skin as a booming voice above him exploded: "Halt or I'll shoot!"

Willie stared first at the floor and then at the wall of the tent. He wasn't sure how long he could keep up his game.

He turned to see the woman rise from the table and sit in a nearby overstuffed chair. He wondered if she was the general's lady.

Burgoyne got up and walked over to the door. He lifted the flap. Looking back at Willie, he asked, "That your beautiful animal?"

Willie bit his bottom lip and said nothing.

Letting the flap fall, the general said, "If you do not speak, I shall have the animal shot and used for food. They tell me horse meat is not at all bad."

"No!" Willie could keep up the pretense no longer.

The general chuckled. "Found your tongue, eh? Nothing like a bit of strategy to help someone open his mouth." He sat back down and poured himself tea from a silver pot. "All right. Stop wasting my time. What's your name and what are you doing in my camp?"

Willie quickly made up a story. It was the only way. If Burgoyne knew him to be a spy, he would be shot. "My name is Willie. I was just admiring your great army. I have never seen so large a body of people. No harm was meant."

The general stared into Willie's face. It caused the boy much discomfort.

"Your father a white man?"

"Yes, but he's dead. My mother was Indian—Seneca. I'm on my way back to the village now."

"How did you learn to speak such good English?"

"Missionaries came to my village."

The batch of lies seemed to satisfy the general. Willie had not known he could lie so easily; the fact rather startled him.

The general spoke to the woman in French, and she began to remove the dishes from the tent.

"How old are you?"

"I have lived fifteen summers."

Burgoyne pointed a well-manicured finger at Willie. "You will not live a sixteenth summer if I catch you around my camp again."

"Yes, sir."

The general snapped his finger and a soldier entered.

"Let the boy go, but give the command to shoot on sight if he's seen around this camp again."

"Yes, sir, General." The soldier shoved Willie out the door.

As he rode out of camp, Willie looked carefully at everything. He could tell his father that the British army was in full strength and getting ready to move out today.

He considered himself lucky to be alive.

CHAPTER TEN

Heartbreak

The sun was unmercifully hot on Willie's naked back. He had ridden hard all morning, trying to put as many miles as possible between him and the British army. The boy had stayed away from the river as much as he could. The tree-buttressed road presented too much of a problem for making any time. Besides, he was afraid of running into the British advance scouts.

A creek shaded by tall sycamores looked inviting. The boy stopped to rest. Lush grass grew thick here, and Running Wind took full advantage of it.

After eating the last of the rations Horace had given him, Willie lay in the shade to rest. Then he sat up and leaned against a boulder, enjoying its coolness on his bare back.

To his right, he watched a black bear lumbering across the sunny shoulders of a mountain. He wondered if she had cubs.

He spied some wild turnips growing nearby and went to get them. He dug the roots up with his knife and rinsed them in the running creek. They were as hot as pepper, but at least they were filling. He lay on his belly and drank from the creek.

After a while, Willie rose and whistled to his horse, who came, still chewing a mouthful of grass.

"You're gonna bust, Running Wind." He stroked the stallion. "We've got to move on. I know how you hate to leave all this good grass, but we got things to do."

They rode for half an hour before Running Wind began to falter. "What's the matter, boy?" Suddenly, the horse was heaving, his great sides going in and out between Willie's legs.

The boy slid off and examined Running Wind's feet, legs and neck. Then he saw it. Bloat! The horse's sides were filled with air. There had been too much of the dark green grass and cold water after a hard ride. "Oh, Running Wind, you're bloated. Oh, no! What'll I do?"

Willie searched his mind for ways to help the stallion. He led the animal to the shade of an overhang. The horse was gasping now and lay down, almost falling.

Willie sat nearby while a helpless feeling engulfed him. He stroked the big head and watched the great eyes roll back.

"Please, don't die, boy!"

He remembered a mare his father had treated for bloat. Karl had punctured the mare's side to let out some of the air. Willie touched the knife at his side. A sick feeling rushed over him.

He rubbed the horse's side. It seemed to grow bigger by the minute.

Heaving a sigh, Willie fought back tears of fright. He wasn't sure he knew just where to stick the knife. Up on his knees now he looked around, hoping frantically that someone would come along to help him, but he was alone. "I can't let you die without at least trying."

He pulled the sharp knife from its scabbard. The sunlight caught it, and the rays bounced off it as if from a mirror. He ran his finger lightly over the blade and fought to keep his hand steady. He bit at his bottom lip until he tasted blood in his mouth.

"Running Wind, you know I love you and would never hurt you if I didn't have to." He wiped the tears with his arm so that he would better see what he was about to undertake.

He sniffed and got a last solid grip on the knife. He aimed at the most swollen area. Taking a deep breath, Willie plunged the knife in and quickly pulled it out. A great *whoosh* of air came out. Willie's eyes widened. Then he sat down on the horse's side and pumped up and down to expel more air. Only a small amount came out. He pumped with his hands until he was weary.

He finally stopped and sat near the horse's head, looking into the glazed eyes. The horse only stirred faintly; he would not even perk his ears.

"We got to go on, Running Wind. You just got to get better!"

One ear went up slightly. Willie swallowed hard. He was so tired of making decisions. But here was another one for him to make. Should he stay with his sick horse or leave him in the shade and go on with his mission?

Willie's young heart ached to stay with his horse, but his head urged him to continue on. Maybe he would find someone along the way who could help his horse.

Once more he stroked the horse between the ears. "I have a job to do. I'll come back here quick as a flash, and I'll find somebody who can make you better in a hurry. You'll see, I'll...."

He paused. The heavy breathing had stopped. He quickly felt everywhere for signs of life. "Running Wind, wake up. Get up now, do you hear me?! Get up!" He screamed at the horse until his voice echoed out over the mountains. "Get up!"

Tears poured freely down his face as he shook the horse violently.

Finally, Willie lay down beside the stallion and put one arm on his neck. With his free hand, he pounded the hard earth and his eyes emptied themselves of their tears.

The decision had been made for him.

———————

Willie did not feel the sharp stones as his bare feet sped over the trail. He scurried down the hillside to where he had left his father and the others. His heart seemed to hold a million thorns and the heaviness in his chest was almost more than he could bear. He wondered how it was that he was able to keep moving toward his destination.

He stopped once to vomit, and then kept going. The sour taste in his mouth caused him to swallow again and again.

He stopped. The area was in view now, but all was silent. No one was here. They had gone on. Of course they went on. They couldn't stay in one spot to wait for him. Night was almost upon him and the boy began to feel fatigue.

He sat on a felled tree and rubbed his palm over a freshly cut stump. He let out a deep sigh and leaned back, looking at the pale moon as it eased over a mountain. He watched the fireflies light up the nearby tree branches. Willie got up and walked down to the river. The water was rushing by as though it had not a care in the world. His mission had been for nothing. There was no one to hear the news he had.

A branch cracked. Tense, Willie reached for his knife before whirling around.

"Willie, that you?"

Horace Cuyler walked up with a grin on his homely face.

"Horace, I'm glad to see you."

Cuyler squeezed the boy's shoulder. "You all right?"

Willie nodded. "Where's my father?"

"They went on ahead, and I stayed to wait for you. Knew you'd be concerned. What'd you find out?"

Willie took a deep breath. He first told about the capture and then about the army headed this way.

"I'd say you one lucky Dutch-Injun to be alive. Some of those men in Burgoyne's army are mighty bloodthirsty."

Willie nodded, thinking of Jane McCrea's murder.

Horace said, "Where's your horse?"

Willie's shoulders sagged as he told him about Running Wind.

Horace shook his head sadly. "I tell you, boy, you've had loads to carry. I'm plumb sorry, but there'll be others."

Willie shook his head. "No, I never want another horse."

Horace squeezed the boy's shoulder again. "Sure you will. No man can get along without a horse, even an old plug like mine."

Willie gave a slight smile. Horace had a beautiful horse. For now, though, the boy was determined that no other horse would ever take Running Wind's place.

Horace slapped his hands on his bony knees and stood up. "Guess we can bed down here for the night. At first light I'm gonna catch up with the regiment and tell them what you learned about Burgoyne's army."

Willie said, "I'll go with you."

Horace shook his head. "No, your pa said you was to go home and wait for him. That battle's going to be one bloody mess, and he don't want you there. Says if he's not back home in two weeks, you are to go to your aunt in Albany. She'll take you in."

Willie shook his head. "No, Horace. I'll never go to my aunt. If something happens to Pa, I'll return to my mother's people."

Horace tilted his head to one side. "Can't stop you thinking like that. But let's just *believe* your father's coming back. He's such a tough old rooster, nothin' can happen to him."

Willie nodded. "I hope you're right. I wish I could go. Can't do no good for the cause at home."

"Yes, you can. Your father said you should make up cartridges from the lead and powder you hid under the floor and get in as much fodder from the field as you can. Winter's comin'."

Disappointment filled Willie's heart, but he nodded his agreement. Just before drifting off to sleep, the boy said, "Thanks for waiting for me, Horace."

He felt Horace squeeze his shoulder.

CHAPTER ELEVEN

Blood Brothers

Willie remembered Horace's instructions as they parted: Stay clear of the path of Burgoyne's army; take to the high country and circle back to your home. You might not be so lucky if you are captured again.

Surely, Willie wanted no part of Burgoyne's army. Also, he avoided going near the place where Running Wind had died. He had no stomach for more pain.

He entered the small valley where the Mueller's place was. As he rounded the bend in the wagon road, another horror met him. The Mueller cabin and stable were burned to the ground. The old mud chimney was all that was left standing—an ugly reminder.

A sinking feeling filled his stomach. He searched the area, praying aloud that he would not learn that his friends had perished there. The cabin must have been torched many days earlier; the ashes were cold, and the surrounding air was clear of the smell of smoke.

He sat on a stump and wondered how much more he could stand.

As he neared his own cabin, frightening thoughts crossed his mind: What if *it* was burned out, too. "Oh, God," he prayed, "please don't let it be gone." He began to run. When he came in sight of the big, sturdy cabin, he heaved a sigh of relief and thanksgiving.

But what was that? A thin trickle of smoke curled from the chimney. Someone was there! Could it be his father? Maybe he had come home by another route. Tories? They had been known to come in and take over homesteads for a time, burning them when they left.

He circled and came up behind the house, hiding in a grove of white birch near the spring. A dog barked. Willie stopped in his tracks. Then a baby cried.

He caught his breath. Could it be? He could contain himself no longer. "Mrs. Mueller, Josh, are you there?"

"Willie, is that you?" It *was* Katrina Mueller.

He laughed aloud. "It's me all right. Thank God you're safe." They stood in the front door and hugged each other. The baby squeezed in between them, giggling at all the commotion. They were all trying to talk at once.

"I thought something terrible had happened to you when I saw your burned-out place."

Katrina laughed and said, "After the Tories burned us out, we came here, thinking you and your father were home. We had no place else to go. I hope you don't mind."

Willie laughed too. "Mind? I'm glad you're here. I so dreaded coming home alone."

Josh, in his somber voice, said, "My pa died."

Willie frowned. "I'm so sorry, Josh. How?"

Katrina answered for Josh, whose trembling mouth did not want to cooperate. "Fever. He was with his regiment up near Ticonderoga. They buried him there. It would have been better if he could have been buried at his home, but it was too far away."

Willie nodded. "It must be hard for both of you." He turned and placed his musket over the fireplace where his grandfather's rifle had been. Once again, a feeling of loss came over him.

Katrina recognized the look and said, "Willie, we must continue to be strong. God would not put on our shoulders something we could not bear."

Willie looked at Katrina's strained face. Only her eyes were bright. He wished he could feel the way she did, but he could not. He just nodded.

They talked until late at night about all that had happened. Everything seemed easier when there was someone with whom to share. The boy was so glad the Muellers were there.

"How did you get away from the Tories?" Willie asked.

Josh shook his head. "It was a real miracle, Ma said. We was gathering fodder when we heard 'em comin' and we hid."

Katrina stroked the baby's head as he played on the floor near her. "It was hard to watch them burn the place we had worked so hard to build and come to love."

Willie saw tears in her eyes. "Friends of the one we had killed?" he asked.

"Yes," Mrs. Mueller answered. "Naturally, we had only the clothes on our backs. I found some cloth in a trunk here and made shirts for the baby and Josh. I'll pay you for it as soon as I can."

Willie shook his head. "No, you won't. My mother wove that cloth. She'd be happy to know that good use has come of it. Use all you want."

How well he remembered his mother sitting at the loom that had belonged to his grandmother. Small in stature, with long, raven-black hair, she had deftly spun thread from the flax grown in their own fields. The thread was then transferred to a big loom where she wove it into cloth. To the young child, it had seemed a long and tedious process, but she must have enjoyed it; the cheerful songs she sang while working used to fill the cabin.

He looked up to see Katrina watching him. As though reading his mind, she said, "My spinning wheel and loom were burned with the cabin."

He nodded and then said thoughtfully, "Mother's are put away in the loft at the stable. Would you like me to get them for you to use while you're here?"

She smiled. "Maybe later, Willie, thank you." She picked up the baby and rocked him.

Suddenly, Willie felt very tired. "Ready to go to bed, Josh?"

Josh yawned and then kissed the baby and his mother goodnight. "Sure am."

Katrina squeezed Willie's hand. "Thank you, Willie, for sharing your home with us."

Willie nodded. "It's good to have you and Josh and Adam here."

The boys climbed the ladder to Willie's loft room.

In spite of all the pain he had experienced, it was good to be home.

Each morning, Willie and Josh went out to hunt or fish for that day. Then they gathered fodder, tying it in bundles and stacking it in the barn. Later, after a long swim in the river, they came home to make cartridges.

Katrina worriedly reminded them: "Be careful of the hot lead—don't get burned."

Willie walked slowly, carrying the heavy pot of boiling lead. Josh wanted to help, so he held the mold steady while Willie poured. The mold was shaped like a strange looking pair of pliers with cutters on one end. The lead hardened quickly. "Tails" of lead were snipped off to be re-melted. Katrina cut the papers.

Into each rolled paper wadding, just the right amount of powder was poured, and then the lead bullet was dropped in. The top of the rolled paper was twisted and a ready-made cartridge was fixed. It was a slow process, but nobody minded.

Josh asked, "How many we gonna make?"

"Many as we have lead and powder for. We're fightin' a war."

Josh looked at him quickly. *"We* are?"

"Sure. There's more to war than killing."

Katrina smiled. "You got some right grown-up notions, Willie Krol."

He smiled. "I can't take credit for that. My good friend Horace said that." He snipped off the end of a lead bullet and dropped it into the bowl with the others.

Katrina finished cutting her papers and picked up the baby to nurse him. Willie thought that the creaking of the rocker was a peaceful sound.

Katrina said, "I guess we need to try and get to Albany to my folks. We can't stay here on you forever."

He jerked around. "It's dangerous in Albany now. Besides, I like having you here."

"Well, we'll stay awhile. Surely, the war won't last that much longer." She placed the sleeping baby on the bed and stirred the rabbit stew. She spooned some yellow cattail flour into the stew to thicken it.

Willie watched her. He remembered entire days spent with his mother collecting the soft, delicate heads of the cattails. The fine flour did not have to be pulverized. Later in the year, they dug the cattail roots, dried them and beat them into a coarser flour. It was a staple food of the Indians.

"I'm glad you showed me about the cattail flour, Willie. A stew without thickening just don't taste good."

Willie smiled. Looking back at his work, he said, "Well, that's the last of the lead." He quickly counted the cartridges. Almost a hundred. "We can do some good with these."

Katrina sighed. "Just pray God we won't have to use them except for hunting food."

Willie had the same hope. He had seen enough death and dying. Little did he know how much more he would have to witness before the war was over for him.

———————

Willie and Joshua climbed a hill and looked around.

"See that other hill, Josh?" He pointed.

"Yeah."

"The river flows just the other side of it."

Josh's mouth hung open in thought. "Where do rivers go, Willie?"

The dark-skinned boy smiled at his friend. "All the way to the ocean."

"Is that far?"

He nodded. "It's far, Josh. Someday, I will go see the ocean."

"You will? Can I go, too? I'm your friend, huh?"

"Yes, you're my friend." He sat down and pulled a sprig of grass, putting it in his mouth thoughtfully.

Josh did exactly the same thing.

Willie had an idea. "Say, Josh. Want to be blood brothers?"

"What do we do?"

"We each cut a little slit in our arms and hold them together and let the blood mix and mingle, and then we're blood brothers forever."

Josh's eyes were wide. "Will it hurt?"

"Naw. Just slit a tiny place."

Willie saw Josh swallow. "All right. I sure want to be your brother."

Willie took his knife and cut a tiny slit in Josh's forearm and then in his own. A small trickle of blood ran from each.

They locked their arms and held them together for a few seconds.

They wiped the blood on soft grass. "Now we're blood brothers, Willie?"

Willie nodded. "That's right."

Josh sighed happily. It warmed Willie to see his special friend so happy.

They started down the hill, and Josh tugged at Willie's arm. "Horses!"

Willie saw them, too—a string of three horses led by one rider.

"Wonder if he found them wild ones or if he stole them?" Willie said.

"Want to ask him?"

Willie bit his bottom lip. "Might as well. There's just one man, and he's got no reason to hurt us."

They half slid and jumped over rocks until they were next to the trail. They yelled at the rider. "Hello, there!"

The man stopped and pointed his rifle in their direction. Josh stepped behind Willie.

"Don't shoot. We mean no harm."

The man was tall and wore ragged clothes. He had a heavy dark beard, but seemed clean enough. A holey, felt hat sat cocked on his head.

Josh eased out from behind Willie and looked into the face of the rider. "Uncle John, is that you?" he said in surprise.

"Josh Mueller! What in tarnation you doing here? Where's your pa and ma?"

He quickly explained. "Pa's dead, Uncle John. Your brother's dead."

"Battle?"

"Fever."

"Mighty bad. I hate losing my brother, but seems death is all around me." His face took on a defeated look.

Josh said, "This here's Willie Krol. We staying at his house since ours was burned out by the Tories."

"Yeah? You a halfbreed, ain't you?"

Willie bristled inside, but said, "My mother was a Seneca Indian, my father is Dutch, and I am an American."

Suddenly, the man roared with laughter. "That's the spirit, boy! I like you for that, Indian or no."

Willie asked, "Where'd you come by them fine horses?"

"I kinda took 'em off some loyalists that burned out my cabin. I tracked 'em down and killed every one of 'em."

Josh stared at his uncle, not knowing how to take the harsh statement.

Willie glanced at the other rifle in the saddle holster and sucked in his breath. It was his grandfather's rifle! The Swiss-German rifle was one of a kind; Pieter Krol had it special-made in Pennsylvania. "Where'd you get that rifle?"

"None of your business."

"Yes, sir, it might be. It belonged to my grandfather who was murdered." He felt his voice crack and swallowed to gain control.

"What's that you say?"

Willie nodded, never taking his eyes off the big man's face.

"Well, I guess it might be some of your business," the man admitted. "I took it off some scalping Injuns a while back." John

Mueller's expression softened somewhat. "I'm sorry, boy. This rifle cost me my wife and son and a burn out. Them Injuns were with the loyalists."

Willie saw the man's mouth twinge at the corners. He realized that Mueller was also having trouble controlling his voice.

Josh watched first one and then the other. He kept shifting his weight and swallowing hard.

"Well, your grandfather won't be needin' it anymore," Mueller finally said.

Willie stared at the man. He did not like the way he felt toward him. Didn't the man understand how badly Willie wanted his grandfather's gun?

Josh finally said, "Uncle John, Willie's my blood brother. You'll give him the rifle someday, huh?

"I will my foot, boy. Didn't you hear what I just said it cost me?"

Josh's blue eyes stared at his uncle. "But keeping the rifle won't bring them back."

Willie was surprised at Josh's reasoning. "It's all right, Josh."

Josh continued, "We got an Indian baby named Adam, Uncle John."

The man made another remark about Indians.

Josh looked perplexed.

Willie felt irritated. His feelings toward the man kept changing. One moment he did not like him, and the next he did. He tried to answer calmly. "The baby needed a mother, and Mrs. Mueller wanted it after her baby died."

The man sighed. "Guess it's just hard for me to think kindly toward Indians, baby or not. I'm tired and I'm sick of death and dying."

Willie nodded. "I am, too. Why don't you come on to the house and see Mrs. Mueller. You can stay long as you like."

John Mueller looked at Willie as though seeing him for the first time. "Thanks, Willie."

It did Willie's heart good to see Katrina's happy face when her dead husband's brother walked into the cabin. As grouchy as he was, the man even touched the baby's head tenderly.

Josh and Willie went out to split wood. They knew that the grown-ups had lots of things to talk about. Willie hoped that John Mueller could work out some way to help Katrina and Josh and Adam.

At the supper table, Katrina told the boys the news. "John is going to take us to Albany until the war is over." Then turning to Willie she added, "That is if you'll come with us. It's been way over two weeks since we've come, and, Willie, your father wanted you to go to Albany. This would be a good chance...."

"I'm sorry, but I can't go to Albany. I have to find my pa. I feel like he needs me."

John Mueller tried to talk around the food in his mouth: "Boy, you can't go runnin' off in the middle of a big battle looking for your pa. You best come with us to your aunt's house."

Willie shook his head. "No, sir. I can't go. I thank you for the offer."

John shook his head. "Can't force him. Iff'n he wants to get killed, he'll just have to go."

Katrina put her hand on Willie's. "I wish you'd reconsider. We'll all come back to the valley after the war. You'd be with folks that care a lot about you, and Josh needs his blood brother."

Willie looked at her hard and then at Josh's pleading eyes. He knew she was right, but something deep inside would not let him go with them. He left the table and went outside to be alone.

Willie watched as John lifted Katrina and the baby up onto one of the horses. He was glad they would be in the care of such a strong person.

Josh hung behind kicking at a pebble with his bare foot. Willie walked up to him. "After the war, Josh, I'll look for you if you don't come back. We're blood brothers and can't lose each other. All right?"

Josh's voice cracked as he replied. "All right, Willie."

A tear rolled down each cheek. Willie grabbed Josh and hugged him. He would never forget the feel of that bony frame and the wet cheek against his.

John said gruffly, but with a tenderness he could not hide, "Come on, boy, let's go. We have a long trip ahead of us."

Josh mounted the remaining horse, and Willie walked up to the horse Katrina and Adam were on. The baby smiled at Willie.

"He's got a good mother." He didn't know what else to say.

"Thank you, Willie. And you, son, are a good person, and I'll pray for your safety every day of my life." She stroked his dark head.

Before John turned his mount around, he reached across the saddle and pulled out the Swiss-German rifle. He handed it to Willie. "I want no bad feelings between us, Willie. Take it. It's yours."

Willie swallowed and took the rifle. He cradled it in his arms like a baby. A good feeling flooded his entire being. "Thank you, Mr. Mueller."

He waved to his friends for as long as he could see them.

———————

The days passed uneventfully. Willie sat on the front porch one afternoon, holding his grandfather's rifle. The September wind blew through the trees, and the giant oaks showed a tinge of color. The days were warm yet, but—a sure sign of the changing season—evenings and nights proved cool.

More than two weeks had passed. Still there was no word from his father. A deep, dark fear crowded the boy's insides.

John Mueller had told of the raging battle on September 19 between Burgoyne's army and the Americans. It had been at a place called Bemis Heights.

Burgoyne had been able to get more troops and supplies from Canada. He led his army across the Hudson River over a pontoon bridge and just waited for battle. General Gates had moved the American troops away from the place Schuyler had selected. The Colonials ended up some nine miles south of the village of Saratoga. Here the river ran through a narrow pass with steep bluffs on the west bank. The bluffs were named Bemis Heights. On these slopes the Colonials had a stronghold which bristled with artillery. Gates felt sure he could block Burgoyne's army forever.

By now, Mueller said, the Americans outnumbered the British; literally thousands had joined the cause after that terrible murder of Jane McCrea. Willie could tell that John Mueller did not like General Gates. Mueller said that Gates underestimated Gentleman Johnny: Burgoyne immediately found even higher slopes on which to place his artillery.

As Burgoyne's army moved their cannon to that still higher ground, Major General Benedict Arnold begged to be allowed to attack the British before they could get their guns in position. Gates didn't like Arnold, so he refused.

Willie had heard lots of stories about Benedict Arnold; he seemed to be everywhere in this war.

Willie sighed. He guessed Gates was jealous of Arnold. But to his young way of thinking, Gates was certainly nobody's idiot. Gates sent Colonel Daniel Morgan and his famous riflemen to oppose the British move. When they ran into trouble, Benedict Arnold could stand it no longer. He rushed into battle to help them. And help them, he did. But when he asked for more reinforcements to end it all, Gates stubbornly refused, even though several thousand Colonials were just waiting for orders to move in. So the battle was won by neither side. Burgoyne lost some six hundred officers and men who could not be replaced. The Americans suffered many losses, too, but theirs could be absorbed better than Burgoyne's.

And now the two armies faced each other. John Mueller had said that there was little more than a mile between them.

A frigid breeze reminded Willie that he was not at Bemis Heights, but still on the front porch, and that the late September sun had set. He stood up and stretched. Aloud, he said, "I just know Pa is somewhere in all that mess and I aim to go look for him."

He planned to leave at first light the next day.

CHAPTER TWELVE

A Rescue
and a New Friend

As the sun brightened the dark valley, Willie packed his shoulder bag for the journey. He made sure to bring along the cartridges, too. Once more, he placed the family's few valuables beneath the floor and pulled the heavy door closed. He started down the trail in a southeasterly direction, glancing at the graves on the hill. He squeezed the Swiss-German rifle, feeling better prepared for what lay ahead of him.

He ran much of the distance, untiringly, for his Indian blood was in command. He sniffed, listened and watched, his senses sharpened like a wild animal's, constantly wary of danger from every direction.

Near the river, he saw the tracks left by armies of men, beasts and wagons. His eyes spied a British canteen. He filled it with water from the rushing river and slung it over his shoulder.

Thunder rolled across the hills and a heavy rain began to fall. He waited under an overhang and hugged himself for warmth. The damp air still smelled of gunpowder. Willie realized that he was probably not too far from the site of the earlier battle, where armies had waited and planned their strategy.

The rain stopped, and Willie continued his journey. Every now and then, he could hear rifle fire in the distance, but no heavy guns. He thought again of Morgan's riflemen and wondered if the shots were from them.

Nightfall was near. It was time to find a safe place to stay for the night.

———————————

As Willie slept, Burgoyne's army was having a taste of frontier fighting. Burgoyne fortified his camp and waited, while the Americans buzzed close, swarming like insects. Morgan's riflemen and the Oneida Indians who had joined Gates gave the British no peace. British troops dared not leave their guarded lines. Sometimes they were not safe even inside the lines. Both day and night, rifle bullets spattered at the British army. Sentries who exposed themselves were picked off by snipers perched high in trees. American patrols were everywhere, firing the periodic rifleshots which Willie had heard.

Burgoyne's army was in trouble. The nights were getting colder and his troops had no winter clothing. Food was scarce: mostly salt pork and flour—and not much of that. The grass had already been cropped off by the horses, so even they began to starve and die. There was no grain inside, and Morgan's riflemen kept the foraging parties bottled up in camp. Things were getting so bad that desertions were common, in spite of the threat of hanging or of receiving 1,000 lashes on the back. But while Burgoyne's army weakened daily, the Americans grew stronger. Burgoyne was a stubborn man, though. To the very end, he believed that the "British never lose ground." He would never even consider retreating to Ticonderoga.

It was a waiting game and Gates, in spite of many faults, knew that his calculations had been correct all along.

A whimpering sound awakened Willie, and he sat up quickly. The sun was still behind the mountains. The morning air was thick and damp. Willie rubbed his eyes and looked about. There it was again; a whimpering sound like a puppy. He walked quietly through the misty woods, following the sound to a burrow in the side of a small hill.

He peered inside and found two wolf cubs. His heart softened. "Hi, there, fellows."

Their toughest baby growl burst forth and Willie laughed softly. "Where's your mother?" He looked all around. "Guess you're like me. Don't have one, huh?" He gently took them from the hole. No longer afraid of this big person with the kind hands, the cubs tried to lick his face.

"You're sure cute little critters."

He sat down nearby and played with the pups, but was ever careful to watch for an angry parent. He had heard his father say that wolves traveled in packs and were often seen near battlefields. He shuddered at the horrible thought.

He decided to put the cubs back in their warm den. Slowly he got to his feet still snuggling the little animals close to his face, enjoying the feel of their soft fur.

Suddenly, a ferocious growl sounded behind him. He jerked around and faced the meanest pair of wolves he could have imagined.

He eased the pups down to the ground and drew his knife. "Just playing with your babies, Mr. and Mrs. Wolf. No harm done. See, they're all right."

The wolves inched their way toward Willie and the cubs. Willie eased away from the cubs to give the parents a chance to see that their young were unharmed.

The mother rushed to the cubs, as Willie put more distance between them and himself. The male wolf continued his "on-guard" stance, snarling and growling. Willie kept backing away. "I don't want to hurt you, just let me go my way."

The mother put the babies back in the den and then rushed back to the side of her mate, snapping and snarling between growls.

Suddenly, the male wolf leaped through the air. Willie jumped to one side, but lost his footing and staggered backward. As he scrambled to get up, the female wolf was on top of him and then the male.

Willie fought at them to get a blow in with the knife. Rolling over quickly, he was able to get up on his knees. He threw down the knife. The noise distracted the wolves. Willie was then able to grab the male wolf by the throat and choke him until he went limp. The mother wolf bit through the boy's shirt at his arms and shoulders. He threw the male aside and concentrated on the female, who now had backed away to prepare for another lunge.

A shot rang out, and the mother wolf ran for the thick woods.

Willie got slowly to his feet, picked up his knife and looked around to see who had fired the gun.

A young man with very blond hair came into the clearing. Dressed in woodsman's clothes, he looked at Willie and grinned. "Looks like you was kind of outnumbered there, my friend."

Willie managed a smile. "I was. Thanks for coming to my rescue." He looked at his torn shirt. Small trickles of blood ran down his right arm.

"What you doing here anyway?" the young man asked.

Willie looked down. Should he tell this man *anything?* He didn't *sound* British. Was he in fact American or British?

When Willie hesitated, the young man said with a sigh, "No use in playing games. I'm George Johnston, and I'm a militia man in the Continental army. And I pray to God you're an American."

Suddenly the male wolf leaped through the air. Willie jumped to one side, but lost his footing and staggered backward. As he scrambled to get up, the female wolf was on top of him and then the male.

Willie's face broke into a grin. "I am. Name's Willie Krol and I'm trying to find my father, Karl Krol. He's fighting somewhere around here."

Willie walked over and picked up his rifle and canteen. He could feel George sizing him up.

"That's all good and well," the soldier finally said, "but what you doing with that British canteen?"

Willie looked down at the canteen and then into the questioning face. It was covered with more freckles than Willie had ever seen. "I found it."

George said nothing but continued to stare, first at Willie and then at the canteen.

Willie turned to go. "Sorry you don't believe it. Thanks again for saving me from the wolves."

The young man laughed. "Whoa, there. Hold on. Didn't say I don't believe you. Just had to be a mite careful. Got anything to eat?"

"No, sorry. Where did you come from? Been fighting?"

They sat down on nearby boulders and George rested his head in his hands. "Fighting like the very devil. Came here after the battle at Fort Stanwix last month."

"Was it a terrible battle?"

George looked up. "Every battle is terrible when men die, and I can say lots died there."

Willie nodded.

George continued. "I tell you, I never seen such bloody fightin'."

"Wish you'd tell me all about it."

George nodded, glad to be in the spotlight. "Sure, I will. Well, this British officer named St. Leger thought he'd just take over Fort Stanwix and then shoot on down to Albany and meet Burgoyne. Didn't know that Stanwix had been all fortified and ready for battle. His army consisted of a mixture of soldiers." He smirked. "If you can call 'em soldiers."

Willie smiled. He thoroughly liked this young man who was a born storyteller. "What kind of mixture?"

"Oh my, there was Redcoats, Tories, Tory Rangers, a few Germans and some Canadians. But mostly, there was Indians. Must have been a thousand Indians."

Willie nodded. He had heard his father say many times that all of Tryon County up in that region was Tory country—very few Patriots.

George sat awhile and then when his story got exciting, he jumped up and walked around, using gestures to better tell his story. "Old St. Leger also had him a little artillery—a couple of six pounder cannon, two three-pounders and four mortars. He thought he could just blow Fort Stanwix away with those guns, but little he knew." He nodded, agreeing with himself, and continued. "Schuyler knew there was danger from the west; that was why he sent the reinforcements to Stanwix; put a mighty fine colonel name of Peter Gansevoort with his Third New York Continentals to take command of the fort. The colonel and his army finished repairs at the fort and were ready for St. Leger."

The excitement of the battle spilled over to Willie, and he found himself holding his breath at times. "Then what?"

"On August 2, St. Leger and his entire force came out of the woods and paraded around the fort hoping to scare 'em into surrender. When the patriots saw those thousand painted Indians, they knew what fate awaited them if they surrendered. They decided to fight to the last man."

Willie could just see it. He felt sorry for the army trapped inside the fort.

"When St. Leger saw how strong the fort was and realized that they weren't going to surrender, he decided to have his army build a road and bring up the artillery. That's when he learned about Nicholas Herkimer and the relief force that was on its way. That was the army I was in.'' George heaved a heavy sigh and continued. ''Little did we know that St. Leger was settin' a trap for us near Oriskany Village. We walked right into an ambush. Fighting was so heavy it almost killed off our whole army. Herkimer's horse was shot from under him and he got it in the leg. They propped him against a tree, and he lit his pipe and gave us our orders just calm as anything.''

Willie asked, ''How'd you get away?''

George looked at Willie a moment and then said, ''We fought our way out of it. Herkimer had us double up behind stumps or trees. Instead of an Indian jumping on a soldier quick as he fired and scalping him, another was ready with the second shot to kill the Indian. He was smart, he was.'' George heaved a sigh.

''Did Herkimer die?''

George tightened his lips and nodded. ''Yeah, later, when they had to take his leg off.'' Willie saw tears in George's eyes. ''Must have been two hundred good men killed in that ambush.''

''Then what, George?''

He nodded. ''Yeah, well that circle of St. Leger's army was still tight as a drum around the fort, but Schuyler was determined not to lose it to the British. He asked for volunteers, and Benedict Arnold jumped up and said he'd do what he could to save Fort Stanwix and did he ever keep his word. He mustered up a sizable army and hurried toward the fort. As always, volunteers flocked to Arnold's side. He's just a natural born leader, he is.''

Willie nodded almost impatiently for George to get on with the story.

''Well, of course, I don't have all the details. I was with the rest of my unit licking my wounds and wishing to get back into the spirit of the fighting once more, but as I know it, Arnold had a plan to get St. Leger's army to scatter." He sighed heavily. "Seems there was this distant relative of Schuyler's by the name of Hon Yost Schuyler, a sort of half-wit or demented soul who was caught doing things which had him sentenced to be hung for treason. Well, Arnold, knowing how the Indians were fearful of insane or half-crazy people, believing them to be prophets or something, he asked this fellow if he'd go into St. Leger's army and tell them a made-up story to get the Indians to scat. If Hon Yost refused, he would be hung, since he was already sentenced to die."

Willie looked at the storyteller. "And?"

"Well, what would you have done, hung or gone along with the ruse?"

Willie laughed. "Think you know the answer to that."

"Yeah, well so did Arnold. So he gets 'em to shoot several holes in the man's coat and then sends him to St. Leger's army. He goes in screaming and howling about this here Benedict Arnold heading their way with three thousand troops. Almost in tears, he tells them how he barely escaped with his life, showing 'em the bullet riddled coat to prove it. Well, these here Indians with all their fear and respect for the insane, never for one minute doubted old Hon Yost. And they scattered in every direction, taking a goodly number of soldiers with 'em." George slapped his thighs and laughed heartily. "That was a sight to behold."

Willie said, "So where did St. Leger go then?"

George shrugged his shoulders. "Back where he came from, I reckon. It's a cinch he didn't go to meet old Burgoyne with the few soldiers he still had left."

Willie sighed. "Boy, that was a smart move, wasn't it?"

"You bet it was. I tell you, Benedict Arnold is a real soldier."

"Sure sounds like he is." Willie got to his feet and picked up his rifle and canteen.

"That's a fine lookin' rifle you got there. Find it, too?" He laughed heartily.

Willie knew that George was teasing him now. He explained that it had been his grandfather's special-made weapon. Then he told him about his grandfather's murder.

George sighed. "That's a pitiful shame. But you're one lucky young fella to have a rifle like that."

"I don't feel so lucky."

Johnston clapped Willie on the shoulder. "Well, don't be discouraged. We gonna find your pa if he's around these parts."

Willie nodded. "I'm obliged for your help."

"Well, wait till we find him before you thank me. Let's head south. The American camp can't be more than a couple of miles from here."

Willie asked, "Where you been since the Fort Stanwix battle?"

"I went by my place to see about things, stayed awhile and then came on here. I'm hoping to take part in the battle to stop Burgoyne. I hear I missed the one they had on the nineteenth."

Willie nodded. "I heard about that one."

George sniffed. "Hear it was at a place called Bemis Heights. I met up with some troops that fought in it. They said Burgoyne's not a mile away from Gate's camp. But just sniper fire's going on now and then. I think they're both gettin' ready for the all-out big one."

Willie agreed and unbuttoned his coat. His head ached from hunger. He looked around for something to eat and spotted a green growth near a rock. He went over with his knife and began digging, while George watched with interest. Up came several turnip roots. Willie wiped the dirt from them on his pants and ate hungrily, offering some to George.

"What's this?"

"Wild turnips. Keep you from starving."

George took the outstretched turnip and bit into it. "Hot, ain't they? But not too bad when you're hungry."

Willie nodded and chewed. "They're not so hot earlier in the year, but they get kind of strong in the fall. Indians eat whatever they can find, you know."

George nodded. "I learned something worthwhile today. Glad we met up."

Willie smiled. He was glad, too. "Maybe they'll have some food when we get to the American camp."

"Oh, they will. Guess you know there's quite a few thousand troops there. Seems everybody around is coming to fight now."

"Maybe the war will be over soon, George." It was more like a question.

"Well, let's hope so. I'd like to get on with living and find me a wife. But I hear tell fightin's going on lots of places besides here."

Willie nodded. He just hoped that his father was all right and that they'd soon find him.

George hoisted his musket to his other shoulder. "Them militiamen I talked with yesterday said to keep due south and I'd run right into Gate's camp. Hope they knew what they was talkin' about."

They walked through the heavy woods. In spite of Willie's discouragement, he still noticed the different colored autumn leaves in the filtered sunlight. He sniffed. "I smell gunpowder."

George sniffed and nodded. "Yep. Probably from that battle at Bemis Heights. It lingers forever it seems."

A wild turkey gobbled, and they froze in their tracks. The two young men looked at each other. It wasn't the season for the mating call of the turkey.

George put his finger to his lips and whispered hoarsely, "Somebody's seen us. Just stand still."

Willie swallowed. Only his eyes moved as he scanned the trees around him, waiting for the turkey call to sound again.

He looked high in a spruce and saw a quick movement of the branches. He motioned to George to stay there, and he moved swiftly and soundlessly through the woods, darting behind trees, but still watching the spruce. He could see a man's legs locked around a sturdy branch, his backside to Willie.

With a commanding voice, Willie said, "If you're an American, you better say so or you're about to hit the ground like a squirrel." He pointed his rifle toward the hiding man.

Laughter exploded from the tree as a young man dressed in a deerskin shirt and britches scaled quickly down the trunk of the tree. He faced his discoverer.

"You just an Indian young'un." He looked quickly at George coming toward him. "And he ain't much more than a young'un."

"You saw us, didn't you?"

"Could have killed you thirty minutes ago."

George asked, "Why didn't you?"

"You didn't walk nor talk like the enemy."

George laughed. "What would the enemy walk like?"

"Like he didn't have no business here. You two walked with purpose. The whole camp knows you're here now."

"Camp?" They both said at once.

"Yeah, I'm one of Morgan's riflemen. Name's David Elerson." He held out his hand.

They shook his hand and introduced themselves. "What you doing in that tree?" George wanted to know.

"Lookin' out across that field over there beyond the forest. Watching for Redcoats."

They told him of their need to get to the American camp.

"Well, come on with me into our camp right now. We got vittles. And I know you hungry. Watched you eatin' that old turnip." He laughed heartily and slapped George on the shoulder.

Willie looked at the man's long rifle. He had heard about Colonel Dan Morgan and his riflemen. "You a sharpshooter?"

David's laughter crackled pleasantly through the woods. "You might say so."

Certainly, Willie could not know that the young man was indeed a sharpshooter; that he was an inseparable companion of the very well-known Timothy Murphy. Together they gave Burgoyne's army fits; they seemed to be everywhere at once, even slipping close enough to the British camp to surprise and capture a sentinel. From him, the riflemen learned the password to get into a British camp, and use it they did. But in time, Willie and George would learn about David Elerson and Timothy Murphy.

The camp was snuggled down in a gully out of the wind. It was almost dusk and the men were doing various chores for the evening meal. Willie's mouth watered at the smell of the food cooking. Some of the men looked up as the three entered the makeshift camp.

A dark-haired young man with piercing eyes looked up from brushing his horse. "Hey, David, who you got there?"

David turned and spoke to his friend. "Hey, Timothy. This pair found *me* in a tree if you can believe that. This Indian lad here would have shot me like a squirrel, too."

Willie felt a bit uncomfortable at his remarks, but not for long. Timothy shook their hands. "Well, if you can find David in a tree, either you're good or he's slipping." Warm laughter filled the air.

David said, "I'd been watching 'em for half an hour. Knew they were good folks."

Timothy laughed.

George said to Timothy, "I heard you got a really special kind of rifle."

The other man didn't answer, but turned and picked up a nearby double-barreled long rifle and handed it to George.

George whistled softly. "Can you imagine that. Don't leave no room for surprises, does it?" He handed it to Willie, who took it carefully and inspected it.

"Can't say I ever seen a double-barreled rifle." He handed it back to Timothy, who polished the barrel with his sleeve.

"No, I 'spect not. There are other double-barreled rifles, but not as light and easy to handle as this one. Had a gunsmith by the name of James Golcher of Easton, Pennsylvania make it for me."

Willie picked up his own rifle and handed it to Timothy. "My grandfather had this one made in Pennsylvania, too, I think."

"Fine looking piece of work. Looks like the same kind of work, too. You lucky to have such a weapon."

Willie nodded. There was that word *lucky* again.

Timothy said, "Well, come on, let's hunt down some food for our guests."

The thick stew and hard bread tasted good. Willie dipped the bread into the stew and ate slowly to make it last. Looking around the camp at the riflemen, he realized that most of the men here were six feet or taller; only Timothy Murphy was somewhat shorter than the others. Willie knew they were the deadliest shots to be found anywhere. He figured, though, that this camp was only a very temporary one to scout from. Willie had heard that Morgan's main camp was near Bemis Heights.

George chewed loudly, thoroughly enjoying the meal. "What kind of Indians are those?"

Willie looked at the Indians who were in Morgan's scouting party. "Oneida, I think."

George swallowed. "I hear they're giving the British a fit too, along with these riflemen."

Willie nodded. "I bet they are. I wonder where Colonel Morgan is."

No sooner had he spoken then a tall man rode into camp on a fine white stallion.

The men came to greet him, and everyone seemed glad he was there. Willie figured it *had* to be the colonel.

George whispered, "Bet that's Colonel Morgan."

Willie nodded. So this was the man Horace had told him about; a man with the uncanny ability to train his men and encourage them to loyalty for the cause.

"We got 'em scared, men," the colonel said in a loud voice. "I just came from headquarters. Burgoyne can't move in either direction. They're calling the first battle a draw, but we're holding the reins."

The men sent up a cheer.

It seemed to take great effort for the colonel to dismount, although the man seemed like a giant. Willie remembered hearing that in Morgan's younger days he had struck an officer. For this, he was sentenced to five hundred lashes on his bare back. It would have killed most men, but he survived, and carried the scars on his back to this day. Another time, in an Indian battle, he had been shot in the neck. More dead than alive, he had still outrun his pursuers and survived. Horace said he suffered from a kind of arthritis from that beating and from all his injuries. Even after all of that, now in his early forties, the colonel was a man of granite.

Timothy Murphy walked up to Dan Morgan and smiled. "Tell us what Granny Gates has on his mind now, Colonel. We been hearing some rumors about him and General Arnold."

Morgan took the cup of coffee someone offered him and leaned back against a tree. He sipped the coffee and then said, "Well, I learned today that when Gates sent in his report about the battle on the nineteenth, he failed to mention Arnold or myself or our regiments."

The men mumbled, and Timothy Murphy said, "Talk about petty!"

Morgan smiled wryly. "That's putting it mildly. Why, if it hadn't been for Arnold and his left wing regiment and us, Burgoyne would surely have broken through." He shook his head. Willie couldn't understand how a general could be so small-minded as not to give credit where it was deserved.

Morgan continued, "Well, it's got some real emotions stirred up in camp." He looked around at the men and spotted Willie and George sitting to one side. "And who have we here?"

David came forward and introduced them.

They shook hands, and Morgan said pleasantly, "You're part Indian, aren't you?"

"Yes, sir, Seneca. My father is a white man, Karl Krol. Do you know him?"

The colonel could see the anxiety in the boy's face. He shook his head sadly. "Name don't ring a bell, but, son there's thousands of men spread all over Bemis Heights and in every gully."

George told Morgan that he had been with Herkimer and Arnold at Fort Stanwix. "I was mighty proud to be a part of it, sir."

"Does me good, George, to see such loyalty." He turned back to Willie. "Your father in the Continental army?"

"No, sir. Militia. Thompson's regiment."

The colonel scratched his head. "Think I saw some of that regiment, but not sure. Why not just stay here tonight and leave at first light for the camp. Ask around. You'll find your father if he's there."

One of the riflemen asked, "We're not going back to camp?"

Morgan shook his head. "Not yet. We'll scout around tomorrow, and then I think you're all going to see some more action. Burgoyne can't sit still too much longer. Rations have been cut and the nights are getting colder. He's just not prepared to hold off."

Willie felt his heart quicken. He hoped that he would find his father before another big battle started.

Later, as Willie lay his head on the knapsack and looked up at the dark sky, he felt lonely. He hugged himself for warmth and listened to George's light snoring nearby.

A tall figure loomed over him suddenly, and Willie sat up. It was Colonel Morgan. He whispered, "Here's a blanket. You'll catch your death of cold on that damp ground."

"Thank you, sir."

Morgan threw another blanket toward the sleeping George. Willie caught it and covered his friend.

"We'll give you some grub come morning to take with you. You can keep the blankets."

"Thank you. We really appreciate your help, sir."

"It's all right." He turned back and said, "You must have a fine father and mother."

Willie swallowed and could only nod his reply. The last sound he heard before dropping off to sleep was the popping of the dying campfire.

CHAPTER THIRTEEN

Running the Gauntlet

The following day found Willie and George in the forest in search of the American camp. According to the map the Colonel had drawn for them, they knew they couldn't be too far from the British camp. Or could they? They heard the yelling and shouts of soldiers felling trees.

Morgan had advised the pair to travel southwest. The sun was their only compass, but it stubbornly refused to shine through the threatening clouds.

After several hours, the two decided that they were practically moving in circles. Without the sun, the map was of little use. By late afternoon, they were picking their way cautiously through heavy woods clothed in scarlet and different hues of oranges and browns. Without knowing it, they were traveling directly toward the German camp which protected the left wing of Burgoyne's army.

"I smell smoke," Willie whispered.

George sniffed. "Wonder if we're near the American camp."

"Don't know. Guess we can follow our noses and see what happens."

"And what if the smoke is from an enemy camp?"

Willie looked closely at his friend. "And what if it's not?"

George shrugged and pulled his floppy hat down over his blond mass of hair. "You're right. Everything's a risk about now, I guess."

They crawled over logs, slid down embankments, jumped gullies and waded creeks. Suddenly, the sky opened, and rain fell in torrents drenching them quickly. Heavy claps of thunder roared like cannons.

George tucked his musket under his coat. It didn't help much. "Wish we were in the mountains so's we could find an overhang to get under."

Strange voices were too near for comfort. They stopped dead still. Together, they whispered, "Germans."

As they turned to leave, they faced two muskets which were pointed right at their bellies. The rain splattered against long bayonets at the ends of their guns. The soldiers wore heavy boots and rain gear.

They muttered something in German, and Willie struggled to understand. The boy knew Dutch, the sister language of German, but still he could not understand the soldiers.

George and Willie raised their hands in surrender. Willie's eyes darted from one stern face to the other. The soldiers spurted out a command. One snatched the canteen from Willie's shoulder, while the other relieved them of their weapons, even their knives.

Willie's heart was racing as he glanced at George. The truth was clear to both. They were in real trouble.

Willie tried his Dutch. "We don't know your language, but we're for the king."

George cried, "Long live the king." He clenched his teeth and muttered, "The blundering king, may he bite his tongue." Then he forced a smile at their captors.

The soldiers motioned and grunted for them to go ahead of them. They did, without another word.

The rain stopped as they walked into the German camp. Water dripped from every tree and bush. In the flickering light of the sheltered campfires, everything had an eerie look.

Several hundred Germans and Indians were in the camp. It was obvious that conditions were not too good. Their once beautiful uniforms were tattered and without buttons or adornments. Many of the Germans were barefoot while some wore stiff, high boots.

The two youths were marched toward a long row of tents and temporary shelters spread over bushes. Slurs were hurled at them from both sides.

George whispered to Willie, "Don't look like no winning army, does it?"

Willie shook his head and again felt compassion rising in his throat for these people so far from home and family, fighting a war which many of them did not understand or care about. His father had told him about the Germans in Burgoyne's army. They were Hessians: German soldiers hired by the British to help fight the war. Then he remembered Horace's words about the enemy being a bear which can devour you, even though you might have pity for it under different circumstances. Willie sighed deeply.

At the door of a large tent stood one of the biggest and meanest looking Wyandot Indians Willie had ever seen. His huge arms were folded across his chest and his eyes pierced Willie's. With an almost perfect British accent, he said, "Halfbreed traitor!"

Willie ignored the insult as he and George were shoved into the tent and onto the ground.

Willie glanced around the tent. Two heavy candles burned on a table where maps were spread out.

The Wyandot glared at the two on the ground. Real fear gripped the boy's heart. He knew George shared his feeling as he looked up at the enormous Indian.

The Indian spat out the words, "What tribe?"

Willie swallowed and then said, "My mother was an Indian princess and my father is a white man." A boiling urge to tear into the big Indian seethed inside of Willie. "Where is your commander?" he asked.

George nudged Willie for silence.

The Wyandot saw the nudge and without warning drew his foot back and kicked George with all his might. George rolled over, holding his side and groaning.

Willie started to his feet. The Indian drew back his foot to kick him but was stopped by a commanding voice, "Aufhalten!"

All eyes went to the door of the tent. A tall German officer stood there with a woman at his side. "Out, get out of here!" the officer said.

The Indian stared coldly at him, then at Willie and George. He turned and left.

Willie looked at the woman. She was short and plump and had a very pretty face with big blue eyes. Her beautiful clothing had a travel-weary look. She sat down in a nearby chair.

"Get up off the ground," the German officer said. "You will have to forgive the heathen Indians. They do not seem to know manners."

Willie nodded and helped George up.

"I am Baron Friedrich von Riedesel."

His accent was heavy but not hard to understand.

"We have very little control over the Indians. If I had my way, I would send them back to their longhouses, so we could handle this war."

Willie knew how important the Indians had been to the British cause. He wondered why the general made such a statement.

The general walked the length of the tent. "But then, you too are Indian." He pointed his long finger almost at the end of Willie's nose.

"My mother was Indian. My father is a white man." He felt tired of saying the same thing over and over.

"Interesting. Are you of a murderous tribe also?"

Willie looked past the general at the woman sitting demurely with folded hands. He thought he detected a smile.

"Seneca."

"And what are you doing with a British canteen?"

Before Willie could answer, George said quickly, "We're for the British. Yes, sir, we're for that wonderful King George."

The general looked into George's face. George was a poor liar.

"You lie. If you were a loyalist, you would not be lurking near my camp."

The woman sighed softly, and the baron looked her way. "May I speak?" she asked.

He nodded. "My wife, the Baroness Frederika von Riedesel."

Her English was not as good as her husband's, but it sounded like a melody to Willie. "You are but a boy, and your companion not much more." She walked over to them, deftly holding her wide skirts. "Whatever are you doing in a dreadful place like this?"

Willie wanted to ask her the same question, but dared not. Instead he said, "I am looking for my father. Please don't ask me any more questions. I don't wish to lie."

The baroness looked at him a moment longer and then turned and looked up at her husband. She whispered something in German, glanced kindly at them and left the tent.

The baron watched her go and then said, "She wants me to feed you and release you, but keep your weapons." He sighed deeply. "But my wife wants to mother the world. We have three beautiful daughters sleeping just yards from here. They all should have stayed home, but my wife insisted." Then, as though sorry for talking so much, he shook his head and sighed. "But I don't see how I can in conscience release you; naturally, you would run to the Americans and tell them all you have seen in this camp."

Willie started to speak, but the baron continued, "Tomorrow, General Burgoyne is calling a meeting here. I will let him decide what to do about you."

Willie sucked in his breath. He could not let Burgoyne find him here—not after the stern warning he had already received.

The Wyandot appeared at the door of the tent and the baron asked rudely, "What do you want?"

The Indian whispered something to the general.

The Hessian commander heaved a great sigh. "You and your kind are bloodthirsty animals. I can see why they call you Black Dog. A more suitable name would be Mad Dog."

His words did not seem to bother the Indian, who nodded nonchalantly and left the tent.

The commander heaved a great sigh. "They want you both to run their gauntlet as punishment for intruding our camp. I suppose I have no alternative but to approve their gruesome request."

Willie's heart raced as he looked at his injured friend. Willie knew he could probably survive, but he was not so sure about George, who knew nothing of Indian gauntlets.

Willie looked at the commander. "I will run the gauntlet twice—once for me and once for my injured friend. If I survive, will you release us then?"

The German officer was clearly impressed. When he did not at once respond, Willie said, almost too boldly, "Will you have to wait for General Burgoyne to make this decision also?"

The baron jerked around at the words. "I make my own decisions. And yes, I will release you if you survive, but I doubt you can run it twice. They are bloodthirsty. But tonight you will be fed and rest until dawn. I will see to that." He stalked from the tent and gave his orders to the guard outside.

Later, in another tent, the two spoke in whispers. "Them Indians will kill you, Willie. I'll run my own gauntlet."

"No, I will make it. You do not know Indian ways. I will run it for you." He clutched George's shoulder to close the subject.

A decent meal of fish and bread was brought to them, and they ate heartily.

George pulled off his shirt, and Willie frowned at the bruised and swollen side. "Feels like he broke a rib," George moaned. "I'd like to meet that dirty dog on even ground."

"There is no even ground for his kind. He'd kill you without blinking an eye," Willie said frankly.

"Maybe. I might have to fight dirty, but I'd like to give it a try."

"Lie down and rest. Tomorrow will be better."

George stretched out on a thin straw mat. He sighed. "They gonna kill you in that gauntlet."

"No, they won't. I ran it many times when I lived in the Indian camp."

"Yeah, but that was just in fun. Those devils out there are playing for real."

Willie smiled slightly. "No. Indian boys run the gauntlet to learn skill in dodging as well as how to stand pain. It was a serious part of our training, even though only switches and cornstalks were used. Whatever's in the hand can usually be dodged. It's more of an ordeal for testing nerves and courage."

When George didn't change his worried expression, Willie laughed. "I'm a very good runner *and* dodger."

George patted Willie's hand. "Still, I'm worried."

"Don't be. I'll be all right, and then they'll let us go."

George moved to get more comfortable. "I hope you're right."

A quiet settled over the camp. A Hessian soldier sang in his native tongue. Willie tried to make out some of the words. It was a sad song. He closed his eyes and asked the Great White Spirit to protect him from danger. Then he slept.

At dawn, two Indians came and led them from the tent. A large group had gathered to take part in the gauntlet.

The morning was cold, and hoarfrost covered the fallen colored leaves.

Willie looked at George walking beside him still wrapped tightly in the blanket. "You any better?"

"Good enough to run my own gauntlet race."

"You still can't straighten all the way up. So it's settled."

The Hessian commander walked toward them. "They have agreed to let you run it twice. You have my word: If you survive, you are free to go. I will have my aide watch over it for fairness. I have no stomach for this type of thing. It's too barbaric."

They watched him walk into another tent nearer the edge of the woods. George sighed. "Guess it wouldn't do any good to make a run for the woods, would it?"

Willie looked at George. "I don't think so," he whispered. "Too many eyes on us right now."

Black Dog walked up next to Willie and rudely jerked off the boy's hat and started to tear away his shirt. Willie pushed the Wyandot's hands away. "Let this be a thing of honor. I can remove my own garments." Their eyes held for a few seconds. Black Dog snarled and then stepped back.

Once more, George pleaded, "Willie, let me..."

A German soldier snatched George back and shoved him against a tree.

Willie took his time, removing his shirt and boots with deliberation. He placed them to one side, all the while building his courage mentally, as he had been taught. He flexed his young shoulders and ran in place for a few seconds.

The crowd tried to rush him, but he turned a deaf ear: another part of his training. Then he eyed the two lines. There were Indians, soldiers and several women and children. Some had heavy sticks, others knives and some, tomahawks. But Willie did not concentrate on the kinds of weapons or clubs, but rather on the distance to the pole at the end.

The participants stood four paces apart. Willie glanced at the onlookers who urged him to begin.

He walked quietly toward the beginning of the waiting and jeering gauntlet, glancing once at George's worried face.

The pole at the end seemed far away, but once there, he would be safe—for the first run.

He took a deep breath and went back several paces to get a running start. He broke into a hard run, and felt the blow of a heavy club landing on his arm. He concentrated on the goal as the blows fell on his shoulders, head and back. He dodged many licks, but there were many he could not avoid. He felt the tip of a whip cutting across his shoulder and cheek, but he kept running, almost falling to his knees as he dodged the thrust of a sharp knife. He felt blood streaming from the whip lash on his face, but ignored it. Gritting his teeth tightly, he ducked his head to ward off a blow, then threw up his arm to knock the toma-hawk from the hand of a grinning Black Dog.

He ran by one scraggly-haired woman, who was bent down holding the stick to trip him, but he jumped over it and at the same time flailed his arm at a spear that was jabbing toward him.

The yells and taunting remarks grew louder as he neared the end of the line. The safety pole was only feet away now. Dizziness flooded his head as he lunged for the pole. He clasped it with both hands and held it firmly, panting to regain his breath. He leaned his face against the hard pole and glanced back. Through the blood running in his eye, he could make out his assailants motioning for him to come back for the second round.

In his half-consciousness, he felt a rough hand jerk him to his feet. He looked into the ugly face of Black Dog. "One more time, Halfbreed. This time, you will not be so lucky."

Willie steadied himself, trying to dismiss everything from his mind and to think of something pleasant to crowd out the horror of this moment. The only thing he could think of was his mother's happy singing as she busied herself around the cabin.

As Black Dog jerked him around to face the gauntlet again, the Hessian commander appeared. "Enough!"

Black Dog sneered. "The deal was for him to run it twice; once for himself and once for the weakling."

Willie took a deep breath and wiped the blood from his eye.

The general put his face right in Black Dog's sneering one. "The boy has survived what most grown men could not. I say let him go. Now!"

Black Dog gave a fake laugh. "You speak out of both sides of your mouth. If *he* does not run, let the weakling run."

He dodged many licks, but there were many he could not avoid. He felt the tip of a whip cutting across his shoulder and cheek, but he kept running.

Willie found his voice. "I will run again. My friend is not a weakling. He is hurt because you chose to kick him."

The general put his hands on his hips. "I am in command here. Neither of them will run it. Your play time is over. Get back to your duties. All of you!"

The gauntlet quickly broke up amid tones of disappointment. Black Dog muttered an insult and spat on the ground. The general chose to ignore him. Instead, he turned to Willie. "My wife will tend to your wounds, and then you and your friend are to leave. If you are caught around here again, you will be shot on sight."

Willie nodded. "Thank you."

"Don't thank me. Thank my kindhearted wife." He nodded curtly to Willie and walked away.

A heavy fog settled over the valley as Willie and George left the camp and headed eastward. Willie thought of Black Dog's parting words: "Look behind every rock and tree, for I will be looking for you to wear your scalp at my side."

George sighed. "I bet that Black Dog or Mad Dog or whatever he called himself, would have called me weakling even if he had been with us at Oriskany."

Willie smiled faintly. "No one but him thought you a weakling, and he is not important."

"Guess you're right. My side's feeling better. I'll be ready to fight by tomorrow."

"The baroness was a very kind lady. She told me a nice story about friendship while she doctored my wounds." Willie touched the cut over his eye.

"What was that?"

"She said long, long ago, there were two very good friends named Damon and Pythias. A mean ruler ordered that Damon had to die by having his head cut off. Well, Pythias said, 'No, please. Damon has a family and needs to live. I will die for him. Just let me go and tend to my affairs first, and I will return and die in his place.' And of course, Damon objected, but Pythias insisted."

Willie picked up a rock and threw it at a tree.

"Go on," George urged. "Then what?"

Willie smiled. "This Pythias hurried off on his horse to get his business in order. But on his way back, the horse stumbled and was crippled and Pythias had to walk. Well, mostly he ran because he knew they'd kill Damon if he wasn't back by nightfall."

George pulled at his hat. "Well, did he make it?"

"You are as impatient as that ruler was, George. I'm trying to remember it right, like the baroness told it. Oh, yes, he ran through the streets screaming and yelling 'cause he saw Damon on his knees with his head locked in that guillotine. The big blade was in mid-air when they saw Pythias running like the wind, yelling for them to stop. Well, when the ruler saw that, he couldn't believe such friendship existed anywhere. He was so touched that he let them both go free."

George stopped walking and looked at Willie. "Kind of like us and the gauntlet, huh?"

Willie smiled. "Kind of."

"You think that Damon and Pythias story was really true or did she make it up?"

"She said it was a story she heard when she was a little girl back in Germany. It's a nice story, whether it's true or not."

"Sure is."

Willie bit his bottom lip in thought. "My father always said friendship was one of the best gifts you could give somebody."

George nodded, "Well, friend, let's walk a mite faster. We ought to be getting to camp soon."

Willie hastened his steps. Maybe now he would find his father or learn some news about him.

CHAPTER FOURTEEN

Journey's End

Colonel Morgan had been right. The American camp was spread out forever, it seemed. Willie's eyes widened at the sight before them. Literally thousands of men milled about, some in snappy uniforms, but most in rough and ragged clothing, with one or more pieces of a uniform to show they were soldiers in the Colonial army.

It felt good to finally be among the Americans. They walked through the throng of loud soldiers, some laughing and singing, others re-telling stories of certain battles.

They walked up to a soldier who was cleaning his musket. "Can you tell us where the general's headquarters are?" George asked.

The soldier looked them over carefully and then pointed. "Go to that grove of trees, and about ten yards or so, you'll see the house where he hides. If you see him give him a good talkin'-to for me."

George lifted an eyebrow. "I take it you don't care for General Gates."

The man placed the musket across his knees. "Not too many do like him after the way he treated General Arnold."

George pretended not to know. "And what was that?"

The young man took a deep breath. "Gates decided to take all the credit for himself in the battle on the nineteenth. Now, he's relieved Arnold of his command and put a little snip of an officer in his place that don't know beans about fighting. That's what Granny Gates did."

"Well, thanks for the information."

"He sure don't like General Gates, does he?" Willie said.

"Don't sound like it. Well, me, I don't give a wink. I'm just gonna join some outfit and help finish off them Redcoats so's I can get back home. I got a heap of firewood to cut before winter sets in."

"If I can't find my pa, I'm gonna join up, too."

George squeezed his shoulder. "I hope you find your papa."

Willie smiled slightly, wishing the same with all his young heart.

They walked to the porch entrance of the big house. A tall soldier with a big chew of tobacco in his cheek was standing there.

"Where do you go to sign up to fight?" George said.

The soldier spat a stream of tobacco juice to one side. "Who's askin'?"

George didn't like the cocky soldier. "You doin' the signing up, are you?"

In a mocking voice, the soldier answered, "No, I ain't doing the signing up."

"Then I guess you just nosy, huh?"

Another soldier walked up. "Down at the bottom of the hill at the big tent." He glared at his tobacco-chewing companion.

George and Willie walked along together for a while. George said, "Willie, my friend, just ask everybody you see about your father. Somebody will help you. I'm gonna leave you here now."

A momentary sadness rushed over Willie. "Reckon we'll see each other again?"

The freckled face burst into a big smile. "Course we will. Can't keep good friends apart."

They shook hands warmly, and each walked his separate way.

Willie asked everyone he saw (anyone, that is, who would pay him any mind) about his father. Some were polite enough, some downright rude, some called him names and others ignored him completely. Feeling disheartened, the boy walked up a small grassy knoll. A woman was there, stirring a big pot over a roaring fire. She held her long skirts back from the blaze with one hand. "Where you goin', young man?"

He smiled slightly and told her his story. She dashed water from a cedar bucket to quiet the fire and then moved to a rough wooden bench nearby. She patted the bench for Willie to sit, too.

He sat down, placing his shoulder bag to one side.

"There's so many thousands of soldiers here, son. But not to worry right now. First, have some food. Looks like you could use a good meal."

"Yes, ma'am, I sure could, and I'm obliged."

She nodded and dipped him some beans cooked with salt pork from the bubbling pot.

Willie took the tin plate, but with his eyes riveted on every person who passed.

The woman wiped her hands on a dirty apron. "I help out at the hospital sometimes and see a lot of folks come and go. Now, tell me again what your pa looks like besides being tall and dark."

Willie put the plate on the bench. "He's kind of slim, and he has a black patch on one eye."

The woman put a finger beside her nose. "Wait a minute. I think I did see a fellow with a hurt leg wearing a black patch. Course, it might not be your pa, so don't get your hopes up."

Despite the warning, Willie's hopes began to rise. "Where? Oh, please show me!"

"One minute. I have to tell you, he is a white man."

Willie grinned. "My father is a white man. My mother was an Indian."

Her wrinkled, sun-baked face brightened. "Well, good. That might just be him. I sure hope so. Let me douse this fire, and we'll go to the hospital tent."

He helped her pick up quickly, and together they strode a hundred yards or more to the big tent which had been set up as a hospital for enlisted men. Another one, across the way, was for officers.

Willie wanted to run, but since he did not want to offend the lady, he forced himself to walk slowly. Once inside the tent, Willie was not prepared for what he saw. A sickening stench of sickness and death filled his nostrils. He fought at the nausea he felt. Cots and thin mattresses were everywhere, with only narrow passageways between them.

The woman saw his expression. "You think it's bad now. You should have seen this place the day of the battle. Things are gettin' better now."

Willie shook his head and swallowed hard. He scanned the injured for his father.

The woman pointed to a far corner. "That's the man with the patch on his eye."

He mumbled his thanks and rushed as fast as he could toward the cot.

"Vater!"

Willie stepped over pallets, walking quickly in his excitement. He bumped the blood-soaked bandage on a man's leg. "Watch it, Injun!"

"Sorry. I'm sorry. Father!"

Those caring for the injured quieted him.

Karl sat up slowly, grinning from ear to ear. "Willie? Am I dreaming? Is that my son?"

They embraced, tears of joy running down both faces.

"You hurt bad, Pa?" Willie asked anxiously.

Karl shook his head. "Better now. Took a ball in my leg; think it splintered the bone." He touched the cut on Willie's forehead.

"It's nothing. I thought you were dead." He wiped the tears on his sleeve.

"Almost, but not quite, Little Eagle."

The word of endearment almost brought another rush of fresh tears. Willie swallowed and sat on the ground, shaking with relief.

Karl put his hand on Willie's head. "I'll get well quicker, now that you're here. I've been worried out of my mind, not knowing if you were all right."

They sat a long time, and Willie brought his father up to date on all that had happened concerning the Muellers, Running Wind, the rifle, the gauntlet in the German camp and his new friend, George.

"Seems you been through more than your share, boy. But your mother used to say that for every experience in our lives, whether good or bad, we grow more. Guess she was right."

Willie nodded.

"Wonder what ever happened to your grandfather's horse?" Karl said thoughtfully.

"Nellie? Probably wild by now."

Karl lay back on his cot and turned toward his son. "No, I don't think so in this short a time. Maybe we can find her after this is over and we go home."

Willie wondered why the concern over Nellie.

Karl smiled. "You know, she might have a colt by now—Running Wind's colt."

Willie straightened up and his eyes widened. "You think so?"

"Highly possible. They got together just before spring. Didn't you notice she was gettin' big?"

He tried to remember how Nellie looked when he turned her loose, but his mind went blank. "Why didn't you tell me?" Willie demanded.

"Wasn't sure she got with colt and didn't want to disappoint you—and then I plumb forgot until now."

A feeling of hope filled the boy. He vowed to search for her if they got back to their valley alive.

Later the doctor came and checked Karl's injury. "Much better. You'll be able to go home in a few days. Have to make you a crutch to get you home on. Only time will tell how much damage was really done to the bone."

They thanked him as he turned to the other wounded men.

"What's going to happen now? Will Burgoyne surrender?" Willie asked.

Karl shook his head vigorously. "Never. Leastwise, I don't think so. Burgoyne's cut off from supplies and fresh troops. He's a fool to chance losing more men with no way to replace them. Winter's coming, and they don't have clothing or food. But knowing his reputation, he'll fight one more battle before he surrenders. War's a game to men like that. Don't think much at all about human lives."

Willie asked. "Who'll take General Arnold's place?"

Karl sat up slowly, grinning from ear to ear. "Willie? Am I dreaming? Is that my son?" They embraced, tears of joy running down both faces.

"Oh, you heard about Gate's stunt?"

He nodded.

"Well, all the troops love Arnold. I expect Learned will replace him. He's a good man, too, just not like Arnold. Why, General Arnold's been in this hospital tent every day since the battle, visiting the injured and telling us all the news of what's goin' on. He's a thoughtful man, he is."

"I feel sorry for the way General Gates treated him."

"Well, he'll make it. There's politics in war same as everything else."

Willie sighed, not knowing much at all about politics. Neither Willie nor his father—nor any of the others in the camp—would have even dreamed that politics would later influence one of the greatest generals in the American army to betray his country. How could they foresee that the very name "Benedict Arnold" would come to *mean* "traitor"?

Willie asked about Horace Cuyler.

Karl laughed aloud. "Old Horace is still around, last I heard. Told me when this war is over, he's coming to our little valley and build a cabin. Think he found him a gal and wants to marry."

Willie smiled. "I'm glad. It'll be good to have another Dutch family around us. I really like him and his bald head."

They laughed together. It felt good.

They looked up into the strong and handsome face of a high ranking officer. A pistol was buckled to one side and a saber to the other. The many buttons on his uniform shone brightly even in the dimly-lit tent.

Karl smiled and straightened up. "General Arnold, I want you to meet my son, William, called Willie for short. Also known as Little Eagle."

A genuine smile crossed the man's face as he held out his hand. "Your father has been worried about you. I'm glad you found each other."

Willie stood quickly and shook his hand, not knowing what to say.

"He tells me you've been through quite a lot."

"Not as much as my father. Everything's going to be good now."

"War is a nasty business, young man, but necessary at times for freedom."

Willie nodded. "Yes, sir. I wish I could be more a part of it."

Arnold put his hands behind his back. "Well, Burgoyne's not finished yet." He raised one eyebrow and said, almost to himself, "Gates has relieved me of my command, but not of my moral responsibility to my men and my country." His pride had been deeply wounded. That pride—and his flair for stylish living—would, in two short years, change the American general into a British spy. For now, though, Arnold *was* a Patriot.

He touched Willie's shoulder. "I don't want you on the battlefield, but I need someone to take care of my horse; to bring him when I beckon and hold him until I need him. Someone reliable. Think you can handle that?"

Chills of happiness raced over Willie's skin. "Yes, sir." He glanced quickly at his father who was smiling and nodding his head approvingly.

"Good. You can come to my tent in the morning and get acquainted with my stallion. From spies, we hear something big is about to happen tomorrow, and I want to be ready."

"Yes, sir, I'll be there early." He wondered what the general had in mind since he had no command. He was soon to find out.

As the general left the tent, he stopped at each cot giving words of encouragement to the men as he walked among them.

Willie spread out the blanket Colonel Morgan had given him. He slept soundly for the first time in a long time. And so did Karl.

Willie was weak-kneed with excitement as he stood behind the fortifications, holding the reins of General Arnold's black stallion.

It was October 7. A second battle was swirling around Freeman's farm. It had its bloody beginning when Burgoyne's army made a last ditch effort to by-pass the American position. General Gates had ordered Morgan's Riflemen to stop them. It was not an easy task.

The day had begun clear and crisp, with the sun shining on the multi-colored foliage of autumn, but after the first volley of shots, smoke filled the battlefield, leaving the visibility very limited. Willie strained to see what was happening. The noise of the cannon and musket fire and yelling of orders almost deafened the boy, but he was determined to do his job and do it well. He kept watching General Arnold pacing back and forth yelling words of encouragement to the men. Willie had heard an argument between Gates and Arnold, but the boy did not understand. Arnold had screamed at the commanding general to send more help for Morgan, and Gates had told Arnold pointblank that he had no business there.

Arnold came to Willie and took the reins from him, nodding curtly as he mounted.

Willie's eyes widened as the general rode up and down behind the lines, almost beside himself as the sounds of battle swelled. Finally, Arnold could stand it no longer. He dug his spurs into his horse's sides and shouted, "Victory or Death!" He burst forth from the American entrenchments and galloped toward the heart of the battle.

Farther down the line of fortification, Gates was told of Arnold's headlong rush into battle. The commanding officer sent one of his aides, Major John Armstrong to catch Arnold and bring him back. Arnold saw him coming and galloped all the harder, with poor Armstrong hot on his tail.

Arnold was a dashing figure as he brandished his long sword over his head and called to the men to follow him. And follow him they did. Yelling and firing, seeming almost cheerful to die, they followed their Pied Piper toward a certain victory.

The fortifications withstood the onslaught and the action moved on to Breymann's Redoubt. The British and German soldiers, weary from hunger and deprivation, were no match for that onslaught of thousands of screaming rebels who had the cause of freedom uppermost in their minds.

Willie moved as close as he dared and strained to see the action through the heavy cloud of black powder. He could dimly make out some Hessians. They knelt among some trees, firing their rifles with precision. Another Hessian company advanced through tall weeds, only to be stopped by the Colonials. Each time the British soldiers to their left knelt to fire, only a few rose from their positions.

Willie ran up and down the line trying to keep Arnold in his sights, but he was unable to. Gunpowder burned his nostrils, and the booming cannon hurt his ears and head. The battle continued forever, it seemed to the boy. Men on both sides dropped like so many leaves from a tree. After what seemed like hours, someone yelled, "Arnold's been shot. His horse was shot from under. He's taken a ball in the leg."

Willie sucked in his breath. He waited for news of what was happening. The men gathered around their leader and brought him safely from the bloody field.

General Fraser had been killed by one of Morgan's men—some said it was Timothy Murphy. Willie heard the soldiers say that Fraser had been a fine British officer. What Arnold was to the Patriots, so had Fraser been to his men.

Finally, the battered British withdrew.

Willie saw them take General Arnold on a litter toward the officer's hospital tent. He lifted a hand to Willie, who forced a smile at the gallant man. Feeling sick and tired, and filled with terror from all the dead and injured, Willie walked slowly up the hill toward the hospital tent.

Karl and Willie talked until late that night after sharing a simple meal of beans, salt pork and bread. They heard some commotion at the front of the tent and someone said excitedly, "They're bringing General Arnold in *here*."

Willie sat up and watched as the general was helped over to a cot nearby. It was uncommon for officers to be with enlisted men. Did Gates kick him out?

General Arnold settled in and then looked over at Karl and Willie. "Wanted to be with my men. They didn't act too happy with me in the officer's tent."

Willie asked, "Does your leg hurt bad?"

"Hurts like the devil. But I gave orders that no matter what, they were not to cut off my leg, as shattered as it is."

Willie felt tears of compassion fill his eyes at the great man's brave words. Then he felt his father's hand on his shoulder.

Early the next morning, General Gates, along with several aides, walked briskly toward Arnold's cot. The stoop-shouldered man in a blue linen frock coat folded his hands in front of him. "You stupid fool!"

Arnold raised himself on one elbow and stared at the angry man.

"Not only did you endanger the lives of all those around you," Gates continued, "but you got yourself shot up. What do you need? A court martial to get you off the battlefield?"

Arnold took a deep breath. "Sir, I received my appointment straight from General George Washington. My responsibility was to my men and my country. God Almighty has not yet relieved me of my moral obligations, nor has General Washington relieved me of my command. You best send your usual pack of lies to Congress and let them decide the issue."

Gates' face was red as a rooster's comb. "I certainly plan to report to Congress and General Washington. As soon as you are able to travel, I want you out of my sight."

"I will leave when I am ready," Arnold said quietly.

Through clenched teeth, Gates informed him, "The battle is over. Burgoyne has withdrawn his troops toward the village of Saratoga. I expect him to surrender in a few days. There's nothing for you to do here."

Arnold smiled cynically, "The battle was won, but no thanks to you. It will go down in history as it truly happened, not as you report it to Congress."

Gates narrowed his eyes at Arnold, turned on his heel and left, his aides following quietly behind him. Both aides gave Arnold a genuinely warm smile as they left.

Willie watched Gates leave the tent, his head high in the air, not bothering to speak to or touch the injured.

Arnold lay back and put his arm over his forehead in thought.

Karl whispered to his son, "You've just witnessed a power struggle between two good men. They just possess different talents and have different sets of values to live by."

Willie listened to his father's words, but still found it hard to believe that Gates was as good a man as Arnold. Maybe he just didn't understand a lot of things. He wished he could think of something to say to make General Arnold feel better, but he could not.

Karl interrupted his thoughts. "We'll be going home soon, son."

Willie nodded and smiled. It would be good to go home.

Willie walked outside the hospital tent to get some fresh air. He strolled up to the fortifications. The battleground was quiet now. The smell of gunpowder still lingered faintly in the crisp morning air.

Once more he pondered his mixed-up feelings. He was glad they had won the battle, knowing it was another step toward freedom from British rule. But he was sad because so many lives on both sides had been lost. It had been hard, too, to see the proud British army on its knees. Willie looked up and down at the line of cannons. They were still manned, just in case Burgoyne tried something foolish. It wasn't too likely, though: The main army had gone on ahead to Saratoga Village.

He whirled around as someone touched his shoulder. "George!"

"Howdy, Willie." They grabbed each other's shoulders in a friendly sort of way.

"Wasn't that some battle?" George said.

Willie nodded. "Did you fight in it?"

George shook his head. "Naw. The outfit I was with was ready, but they didn't need us after all."

"I found my pa." Willie told his friend about Karl's injury and all that had happened.

George's face brightened. "That's really good news. Well, we got 'em whupped now. They say this here battle will change the course of the war and that France will come in and help us wrap it all up."

Willie sighed, "I'm glad. I'm so tired of all this. My father and I will be going home tomorrow."

"Me, too. Gonna marry me a woman and get on with living."

Willie thought for a moment. He looked to the far corner of the field where a large grave was being dug. Many soldiers would be buried in the one grave. They wouldn't be getting on with living as he and George would.

George broke into his thoughts. "I'm going now, Willie. I might see you before long. I hear there's good land in that valley of yours. Might just settle down near there." Every freckle seemed to stand out anew on his honest face.

Willie laughed aloud. "Good. Maybe someday we'll have a regular village."

George pulled up his loose pants and sniffed. "You ain't the only one who's Dutch, you know. My ma's maiden name is Stuyvesant."

"How about that? But where'd you get all those freckles?"

"I've also got some Irish blood in me." He laughed.

Willie grinned. "Well, we'd be mighty proud to have you."

Willie stood awhile after his friend had left, still thinking of all that had happened. He would be glad indeed to get back home.

CHAPTER FIFTEEN

A New Beginning

Willie and Josh walked along Buster Creek looking for smelt. The small silvery fish, when cleaned and fried a golden brown, were good eating, bones and all. Each spring, they came by swarms out of the rivers and lakes to spawn in creeks and branches. It usually didn't take long for the boys to get enough for a meal. Then they would dry the surplus to store up for later months.

Willie pushed his hair back from his face as he peered into the water. "Guess it's too early for them to run."

Josh threw a pebble into the stream. "I'm mighty hungry for smelt. Hurry up, smelt!" He laughed at his own silliness and Willie joined in. How good it was to have the Muellers back as neighbors. Karl had only a slight limp now and had been able to help rebuild the Mueller cabin.

Willie stepped over a big rock. "Glad your Uncle John married your mother?"

He grinned. "Shucks, yes. He's good to me and Ma and Adam." Then as an afterthought, he said, "But he talks loud sometimes."

"Well, I bet his bark is worse than his bite."

His mouth open, Josh looked at Willie as he let the words sink in. Then a smile crossed the younger boy's simple face. "Oh, I get it. He barks but he don't bite." He laughed heartily, and Willie joined in.

"I wonder if we'll find Nellie." Willie let out a sigh. "And if she has a colt." He thought of what Horace had said about his wanting another horse after Running Wind. He knew now that Horace had been right. He desperately wanted Nellie to have that colt. But he would not allow himself to have too many hopes.

"Well, we won't find her by looking for smelt that ain't here."

Willie laughed at his friend's way of expressing himself. "You're right; let's go."

They jumped the stream at a narrow point and headed for the valley beyond the mountain where they had last seen the wild horses.

Willie moved his coil of rope and looked at the snow which still clung to the ground in shady spots. The trees were budding and the yellow-orange heads of crocuses brightened the world around them. Willie sniffed the fresh smell of spring.

The boys heard the ringing of axes felling trees for new houses all around the valley. Willie's friend, George Johnston, had found himself a wife indeed. She had a timid smile and loved her freckle-faced husband. They would be moving into their new home soon, along with George's mother-in-law, a handsome widow lady who found Willie's father very attractive. Willie wondered how Karl felt about her.

Horace had married a plump lady with a quick smile who figured that God had made Horace just for her. Willie smiled to himself. Horace refused to take off his cap even at mealtime, since his wife was making him let his hair grow back.

The Dutch settlement was becoming a reality. The war was not over yet, but their little valley was quiet and peaceful. Willie let out a contented sigh.

By now they were near the clearing. Willie scanned the green meadow with keen eyes. He nudged Josh's side. "There, at the end of the field. There they are!"

Josh whispered hoarsely, "I see 'em."

"There's six."

"Do you see Nellie?"

Willie shook his head. "Not sure." He paused, then said, "Yep, by crackie, I *do* see her."

"You see a colt?"

"No, but let's move in closer."

They moved quickly down through the rocks and stood at the edge of the field.

Josh yelled excitedly, "There's the stallion!" His voice rang over the valley.

The white stallion quickly rounded up his mares and led them through the narrow opening at the end. All except one.

"Josh, you did it now," Willie said, disappointed.

Josh was ashamed. "I'm sorry. I just got excited."

"It's all right. You didn't mean to."

Willie looked at the mare that had refused to go. "It's Nellie!"

The stallion came back for her, but she refused to go even when he bit her neck. He made a commanding sound, bumping against her, but she stood her ground and did not move.

Willie looked everywhere, hoping to see the colt, but did not. He fought back his disappointment as the stallion gave up and ran to his other mares.

"Stay behind me, Josh. She might run."

They walked slowly toward Nellie, whose ears pricked straight up as she eyed them.

Willie held out his hand. "Nellie, it's me. Remember me?" He turned to Josh. "Go quickly and stand by the opening so she won't run out."

The boy moved swiftly to guard the only exit.

Nellie backed away a bit.

"Come on, girl. You can come home now."

She snorted, looking at a large boulder to her right. Willie glanced over but saw nothing.

The mare edged near the boulder, jerking her head up and down and making a funny, grunting sound.

"What's the matter, Nellie? I know you remember me or else you would have left with the other mares." Why was she acting so strange, he wondered. Was something behind that boulder? The boy's heart began to race. Could it be?

Suddenly, Nellie ran to the boulder and put her head behind it. Seconds later, out walked a long-legged black colt with a white streak on its face.

Willie fought back a yell. He wanted to beat the earth with joy, but instead he held his breath and stood perfectly still with a silly smile on his face.

Josh said in a loud whisper, "She has a baby, Willie."

Willie nodded. He could not stop smiling as he watched the colt nudging hungrily at its mother.

Willie was beside the mare now, rubbing her neck and face. "You have Running Wind's baby, and it's a boy. He looks like a tiny Running Wind."

He ached to touch the colt, who turned, milk on its mouth, to look at Willie, and then went back to sucking. The colt's long legs were stretched out behind him in total contentment.

Josh walked up slowly. "Ain't it pretty?"

Willie nodded and looked at Josh, who had tears of happiness on his honest face.

Willie gently slipped the rope over Nellie's neck. They walked out of the valley with the colt tripping spryly beside its mother. Willie thought to himself, when he's older I'll train him just like I did Running Wind. Another Running Wind. No, he would not be another Running Wind. There could be only one. "What'll we name him, Josh?"

Josh looked at the dark rain clouds gathering for a spring rain. Then a clap of thunder sounded. Josh put his hand to his ears and smiled. "How about Black Thunder?"

Willie repeated it. "Black Thunder. I like that. You just named him for me."

Josh beamed happily, glad to be a part of this moment with his blood brother.

A sprinkle of rain began falling, and they walked faster.

Willie heard the cry of an eagle soaring toward the top of a nearby mountain. "The eagle's come back, Josh," Willie remarked. "I bet it has some little eagles in that nest."

Josh giggled and poked Willie's shoulder with a long finger. *"You* Little Eagle." He pointed to the eagle's nest. *"They* little eagles."

Willie smiled and nodded. He put his arm around his friend's shoulder as they neared the house and barn in the pouring rain. It did not matter that they were soaked clear through. Nothing could dampen Willie's happiness.

 **auline** *BOOKS & MEDIA*

ALASKA
750 West 5th Ave., Anchorage, AK 99501; 907-272-8183

CALIFORNIA
3908 Sepulveda Blvd., Culver City, CA 90230; 310-397-8676
5945 Balboa Ave., San Diego, CA 92111; 619-565-9181
46 Geary Street, San Francisco, CA 94108; 415-781-5180

FLORIDA
145 S.W. 107th Ave., Miami, FL 33174; 305-559-6715

HAWAII
1143 Bishop Street, Honolulu, HI 96813; 808-521-2731

ILLINOIS
172 North Michigan Ave., Chicago, IL 60601; 312-346-4228

LOUISIANA
4403 Veterans Memorial Blvd., Metairie, LA 70006; 504-887-7631

MASSACHUSETTS
50 St. Paul's Ave., Jamaica Plain, Boston, MA 02130; 617-522-8911
Rte. 1, 885 Providence Hwy., Dedham, MA 02026; 617-326-5385

MISSOURI
9804 Watson Rd., St. Louis, MO 63126; 314-965-3512

NEW JERSEY
561 U.S. Route 1, Wick Plaza, Edison, NJ 08817; 908-572-1200

NEW YORK
150 East 52nd Street, New York, NY 10022; 212-754-1110
78 Fort Place, Staten Island, NY 10301; 718-447-5071

OHIO
2105 Ontario Street, Cleveland, OH 44115; 216-621-9427

PENNSYLVANIA
Northeast Shopping Center, 9171-A Roosevelt Blvd., Philadelphia, PA
19114; 215-676-9494

SOUTH CAROLINA
243 King Street, Charleston, SC 29401; 803-577-0175

TENNESSEE
4811 Poplar Ave., Memphis, TN 38117; 901-761-2987

TEXAS
114 Main Plaza, San Antonio, TX 78205; 210-224-8101

VIRGINIA
1025 King Street, Alexandria, VA 22314; 703-549-3806

CANADA
3022 Dufferin Street, Toronto, Ontario, Canada M6B 3T5; 416-781-9131